Nobody's Prey

Jenn Mumma

Kansas City, MO Metro area, USA

Instagram: Jenn_Mumma_Author Jenn_Mumma

Facebook: Jenn Mumma-Author@jennmummaauthor

Copyright: Jennifer Mumma

Cover Design: Jennifer Mumma

Publisher: All rights reserved. No part of this publication may be reproduced or transmitted in any form or by any means, electronic or mechanical, including photocopy, recording, or any information storage or retrieval system without the author's prior written permission.

Table of Contents

Dedication I
Acknowledgement II
Preface III
WORDS OF PRAISE ABOUT THE AUTHOR IV
Chapter 1: Sweet 16 1
Chapter 2: A Must Needed Break-up 18
Chapter 3: School 28
Chapter 4: I'm Being Stalked 41
Chapter 5: He's Escalating 51
Chapter 6: A New Love 66
Chapter 7: Summertime at the Lake 85
Chapter 8: Stalker Strikes Again 100
Chapter 9: Levi attacked 116
Chapter 10: Nobody's Prey 134
Chapter 11: ICU 148
Chapter 12: Recovery 168
Chapter 13: The Story Unfolds 183
Chapter 14: Levi 195
Chapter 15: Abducted 204
Chapter 16: The Search Continues 219
Chapter 17: Imprisoned 229
Chapter 18: The Great Escape 243
Chapter 19: The Search 249
Chapter 20: I'm Rescued 252
About Stalking 260
About the Author 265

Dedication

This book is dedicated to all my fellow stalking victims (I don't like that word; we aren't victims; we are survivors) and those who lost their lives due to a stalker's unhealthy obsession. If you are currently being stalked, please visit the back of my book for some information and ways to get help. This is good to read for anybody because you might be stalked later in life, God forbid.

Acknowledgement

First and foremost, I thank God for freeing me of so many demons and protecting me, and for Jesus, my savior for his work on the cross. I want to acknowledge my husband for always being so supportive, and he's there for me no matter what. He always supports me in everything I do, which means everything to me. I want to thank the Warrensburg Police Department for being so amazing through this ordeal. And "Officer John," who unfortunately can't be named in this book. I'd like to thank my family as well for always being there for me and supporting me.

Preface

This book was dreamed up by my actual stalker experience when I was 16 and 17-years-old. Though this is fiction, it started as NON fiction. But, again, this book is FICTION, but it was brought to life through real events from a young age. I went through things no 16-year-old should have to. In the back, please read about stalking so you can protect yourself if you have a stalker and hopefully end it before it escalates, or just to know what to do just in case one day a stalker targets you.

WORDS OF PRAISE ABOUT THE AUTHOR

"Jenn is the kind of friend everyone hopes to have–loyal, compassionate, and always there when you need her. As an author, her intelligence and dedication shine through in every word she writes, weaving stories that captivate and inspire. Her creativity is matched only by her tenacity; whether facing writer's block, or a challenging deadline, Jenn approaches every obstacle with patience and resolve. Beyond her literary achievements, she's a steadfast confidante and a source of wisdom and encouragement. Being her friend means being truly understood, supported, and valued–a testament to the warmth and depth of her character."

~Laura Jones

"Jenn is a newly passionate writer who has experienced lots of ups and downs in life. Through perseverance, self reflection, and a relentless pursuit of growth, she has successfully navigated the obstacles that once held her back. Drawing from personal experience, Jenn writes to inspire others who find themselves in similar situations, offering practical advice and encouraging words for those ready to push through their own challenges. Her story is a testament to the power of resilience and the belief that no matter how rough life may seem, there's always a way forward."

~**Maeghan Comfort**

"Jenn's life has been defined by resilience, facing each challenge with an unwavering spirit. Her journey of overcoming adversity is a testament to her strength and determination. With faith as her anchor and writing as her newfound voice, she is courageously navigating the path to personal freedom, inspiring others along the way."

~**Angela Cummins**

Jennifer's life is a shining testament to the transformative power of resilience, fueled by her unshakeable determination in the face of adversity. Her journey radiates strength and unwavering purpose. Grounded in faith and expressed through the healing art of writing, she courageously charts a path toward liberating self-discovery, leaving an enduring legacy of inspiration for all those around her"

~**@Luxelife9 -Marilyne Nix**

Opening Page Nobody's Prey

Help Me! Please, somebody, Help!

I wanted to scream, but I couldn't. I looked down at my abdomen and saw all the blood; it was running down my shirt and my jeans. I needed something to stop the bleeding. I could taste the blood in my mouth. *I'm going to die, right here* and now I thought while I tried to stop the bleeding. I looked up at him, and he was smiling, thoroughly enjoying watching me die. He had a dagger. He just wanted to watch the end of the show. The end of my life. Everything that he's done started racing through my head. Every act to get my attention. I'm trying to figure out why. Why me? What did I do to this guy for this to happen?

I had to turn my thinking to survival quickly. I'm not going to let this psycho get any further gratification, and I tried to run. It was more like a speed walk, but he followed me.

Then he smugly said, "Where do you think you are going, Mac?" as he stalked me like I was his prey, with the dagger in his hand, ready to slaughter me.

I'm nobody's prey, I told myself.

I immediately went into survival mode. I was trying to get somewhere where there was a weapon of some kind without him seeing me grab it. I grabbed a towel off the kitchen counter of our farmhouse-decorated kitchen. It was my mom's favorite towel with cows and milk canteens patterned all over it. I took the towel and pushed it hard on my abdomen. It slowed down some of the bleeding, but not all. I turned the corner from our kitchen to the dining room. I was in such a haze I could barely see straight.

My dad's gun, I thought.

He keeps it loaded in the lower drawer of the coffee table. I had to get to it. I now only focused on getting to the coffee table. I was starting to get light-headed, but I fought it. I pretended to fall to the ground so I could crawl, I needed to be low to the ground to get to my dad's gun. Then he kicked me from behind, and I was laid out on the carpet. I cried out in pain, but I had to get back up and crawl around the side of the coffee table because that's where my dad's gun was.

Please be unlocked, I begged God. The drawer must be unlocked, or I'm going to die.

I just had to stay conscious. His dagger isn't going to win against my gun. I wasn't very confident in my aim under these conditions, but hitting him at least once would put us on equal ground.

The way he looked at me was so evil. He cocked his head from side to side like a dog, thern went from having a puzzled face to a face full of enjoyment. He smiled and said, "Your life is in my hands, Mac. How does that feel?"

I just ignored him, which pissed him off. He kicked me in the stomach, and I screamed! "How does that feel?" He repeated.

"It feels awesome!" I replied sarcastically.

Then he grabbed me by my hair again and threw my head down. *OK, Mac, quit pissing him off.* I had to stay focused. If I can't get that gun, my life will be over.

I thought of my parents, Levi, my amazing boyfriend, my sister, my bestie, Mandi. Their faces flooded my mind. I needed to survive. For them. I prayed to God that I could hit him with every shot! I was there; now was the time. This would be life or death. I reached for the handle on the drawer of the coffee table and pulled it.

Chapter 1: Sweet 16

It was finally the day. The day I turned 16! All I could think of was getting my driver's license. To me, that means pure freedom! In addition to that, I'm hoping for a huge party. You know, sweet sixteen and all. A huge surprise type one. A day full of possibilities. I usually don't care about my birthday, but this one was different, I'm 16! My mom woke me up with a donut and she put a candle in it. "Rise and shine, Makayla." She said. She calls me Makayla, but I go by Mac. I wished to pass my driver's test and blew out the candle. Then I ate my favorite donut, a long john filled with cream. Yummy!

I got up, hopped in the shower, and then dressed for the day. I picked an outfit that said, "I'm a responsible teenager."

We'd be leaving soon to take my driver's test and I couldn't get my hair dried fast enough. I was so excited. Drying my hair has always taken forever because it is so long and thick. Michelle, my older sister, was banging on the door to get into the bathroom so she could get a shower. I thought she'd just have to wait to take her turn. "I'll be out in a minute," I screamed at her. I unplugged my straightener and brought it into my bedroom so she could get in the shower. Then she said, "Happy birthday, by the way," and hugged me and apologized for being impatient.

Later that morning, right when the DMV opened, my mom and I headed to the entrance where I would take my driving test. I passed the written test already, so I couldn't wait to pass the physical driving part!

I signed the check-in sheet to secure my spot in line while we waited and that's what we did. Wait, wait, wait. Then finally, they called my name, "Makayla Jackson."

Yes! I screamed in my head.

We got in the car, and I started driving. I did pretty well until the parallel parking part. I couldn't parallel park, so I failed the test.

Dang, like really lady? I said to myself. *Well, happy birthday to me,* I thought sarcastically.

My mom took me to school and signed me in. I was halfway through my school day. I told my friends about the failure at lunch, and they said I'd get it next time. I only had a couple of friends in school. Most of my friends had already graduated. I was the youngest in my class because of my birthday. Also, I skipped kindergarten because the school said I was too smart, so they moved me to first grade.

After school, I got on the bus and headed home. I had to work tonight, and I had a ton of studying and homework to do.

To add to my crummy day, the big sweet sixteen party I was hoping for didn't happen. At first, I thought it would just be a huge surprise, like pretending I wasn't having a party, but that wasn't it. I was bummed for a bit, but I had a lot to do, so I just brushed it off.

I got off work at Sonic at eight pm, and I finished my homework before I went to work. When I got home from work, I took a shower, and then I got all dressed up and spent forever curling my hair. I stood at 5 '10 and was pretty lean. I got a workout at my job and worked out at home or the gym. I loved running and had built up some muscle in my legs. The elliptical and rowing machines were my go-to, and the weight machines for harder muscle work.

I rummaged through my closet to find the perfect outfit to show off my physique. I called a couple of my girlfriends to see if they were ready. Mandi picked me up, and the rest of the crew were going to meet at the bowling alley to throw some balls for a couple of hours and eat the bowling alley's amazing cheese fries! They closed at midnight. My parents usually didn't let me stay out that late, but it was my birthday, so they let me.

My best friend Mandi bought me a slice of pie, pumpkin, my favorite. She put a candle in it that she brought from home. She was gorgeous. I was jealous of her long blonde hair with the perfect natural waves. Mine was half wavy and half straight, so I had to either curl my hair or straighten it. She was only about an inch shorter than me. She was fit and worked out a lot with me. You could see that she worked out from the muscle in her arms and back and her four pack abs and defined thighs.

I felt so loved; she was so sweet and truly my best friend. "Should we light it?" she asked. I laughed and said, "why not? I'll blow it out fast."

But first, Mandi, Kaye, and Misty decided they needed to sing Happy Birthday to me.

NOOOOO, I thought.

As they started singing, all the guys in the lane next to us that we were flirting with joined in. I was so embarrassed! After they finished singing, I smiled, made a quick wish, and blew out the candle. The guys asked what birthday this was. I said, "Haven't you been taught never to ask a lady her age." We all started laughing.

All my friends had gifts for me. Mandi got me this beautiful blouse she saw me eyeballing at the mall two weeks ago. I gave her a big hug! Kaye got me a gag gift. It was about twenty tubes of nail glue! Also, a pamper-me set with a sleep mask, hair mask, body scrub, and lotion from my favorite store. I gave her a big hug, too.

Kaye was one of my other good friends. Kaye's dad was in the military. We met in Arkansas in middle school, and her dad just got stationed here at Whiteman! We were so excited to be together again. She still had long brown hair, big blue eyes, and she was gorgeous. Her features had definitely changed, as I'm sure mine had, too. She was fit and toned. She always looked polished.

Back when we were living in Arkansas, this one time we were at her house, home alone, back when we were 14. We accidentally broke her Christmas tree, and she thought it'd be a good idea to try to fix it with fake fingernail glue. Hence, the gag gift! Soon, the fumes started, and the fire alarm started going off so we called 911. I kept trying to get her out of the house, but she couldn't get her cat. Her cat kept running off. Eventually, I just grabbed her, and we left her house. The fire department showed up and said everything was okay, but she only cared about how hot the firefighters were. Needless to say, her parents were not pleased. She loved flirting way more than any of us. She was a genuine, boy-crazy girl, and also liked older men, but way older men. She had a beautiful smile and was always warm and welcoming to everyone. Total social butterfly.

Misty got me a desk stationary set. She knew how much I loved anything paper! It was a beautiful set. I couldn't wait to use it! I hugged her and thanked everyone for their gifts! "It's your sweet 16," Mandi said, "We had to make it special!" "Don't say that too loud," I laughed.

Misty was a bit more reserved. She was in the class ahead of me. She had a short blonde bob hairstyle that looked amazing on her and framed her face. She was a good friend of mine, and she worked with me at Sonic. That's how we met. She was super sweet. But not quite as boy-crazy as we all were. She had just recently broken up with her boyfriend, which was a good thing because he was a jerk.

Unfortunately, Mandi and I didn't have any classes together, but we made up for that after school. We liked hanging out at the bowling alley anyway because of all the cute guys, especially the Airmen. We could go to the base bowling alley because both our dads were in the military. And at this bowling alley, the guys were mostly Airmen. It also wasn't smokey like the off-base bowling alley because smoking wasn't allowed, which kind of sucked. After all, I smoked, but it was nice for it not to be super smokey. I didn't mind going outside here and there for a cigarette. Plus, the music was almost always top hits, the kind of music we love, and they had super cool lighting and fantastic food.

I told Mandi about failing my test because I couldn't parallel park, and just like that, we were headed out the door. I was a bit younger than her, and she had her license. And even though my permit said I had to be with someone who was 18, she decided to teach me how to parallel park. That's my Mandi.

We told the other girls we'd be right back, so Kaye and Misty saved our lanes and kept bowling. I got in her car, and she got in the passenger seat. We found an empty spot. She told me to drive next to the car in front of me, and taught me how to move the wheel to reverse between the car behind me and into the empty spot I was trying to park in. She made it sound so easy. I didn't make it the first time, so I tried again. I turned the wheel much more this time and then turned it in the other direction and BAAM, I was parallel parked! It took me about 15 minutes, but I can parallel park now. I am so excited to take my next test. I thanked Mandi probably a hundred times.

We hung out a bit longer and flirted with the guys there while we bowled. The guys were all probably two or three years older than us, I don't think they knew we were 16 and 17-year-olds, or maybe they didn't care. I guess I like older guys, and my friends did, too. The guys our age were boring and immature. After we finished our games and chowed down our cheese fries and drank our sodas, we headed to my house to hang out. It was late, even for a weekend, but my parents were cool about it since it was my birthday. My friends' parents were too.

Boys had always been the topic of discussion, but today, we talked about school and colleges and how much fun it would be because we all wanted to go to the same college to stay together. I was partial to going on the coast, and Mandi didn't really care just as long as they had a good nursing program. So, we were on the hunt.

About two hours had passed, and everyone needed to head home. Mandi, Kaye, and Misty, all drove themselves home. I was the only one without a driver's license. But not for long!

After a few days, I had my second driving test, and I failed again. This time I almost caused an accident. It wasn't fair, either. There was this really awkward intersection and it looked like you could just keep going straight. As I approached it, she told me to keep going straight, so I did, but I was supposed to yield to another car and they almost hit us. When she told me I failed because I almost caused an accident and we could head back, I told her I kept going forward because she said to keep going straight. She looked at me with a snarky face and said, "Don't try to put this on me." UGH…The third time's a charm, right?

I had to work after that, and unfortunately, I could not drive myself. My mom had to, as usual, thus the reason I needed my license. I was tired of my parents driving me everywhere, and I'm sure they were too. I already had a car, it was the one my sister had driven. We got the car from my grandma for free and it was being passed down to me. It was an old, ugly gold Impala, and it was like a steel boat on the road. I was already looking for my new car because I didn't want to drive that one.

After about a week, I came back to retake the test. I was so scared to fail again. I think I only have three chances, I can't remember, but I had to pass. I wanted to drive. I wanted freedom! I walked in there and signed that silly clipboard again and waited, waited, waited. Finally, they called my name, "Makayla Jackson, you're up."

My first two driving graders, I guess I could call them, were female. This time I had a male. He was so much nicer than the last two. I drove, parallel parked, and I didn't almost cause an accident. He was chatty, unlike the other "judges". Not overly so I could concentrate, but we had a conversation about school and whether I had made a career choice yet. He said he never thought he'd be doing this job. He went to school to be an accountant. But after all the schooling for it, it no longer interested him.

The drive was over, and I asked how I did. He said I did great. I said, "But did I pass?" He said, "you'll find out soon enough," with a big grin on his face. I had a really good feeling I killed it this time!

I waited about 20 minutes for the news, I finally got the news that I passed the driving part and needed to wait back on the other side of the DMV to get my picture and all the info for my driver's license! Then, my license would come in the mail. I had a paper copy to hold me off.

Did I say I got my license?!

After my mom and I got home, I wanted to go cruise around. I feel so free now. I think all 16-year-olds think that way. All except my sister. After she turned 16, she waited months before she got her license. I thought she was crazy because I wanted mine so bad. We are 21 months apart, so I was close when she turned 16.

My mom had a black convertible Mustang, and I asked her if I could drive it around for a little bit. She said yes and asked me to be careful, so I drove around for a bit with the top down. I texted Mandi that I was headed there and asked if she wanted to cruise around, and she texted back, "heck yea."

I drove to Mandi's house, and she hopped in the passenger seat, and I cruised around some more. We got a lot of looks from some guys. My hair was flying in the wind, getting all knotted up, until Mandi gave me a hair tie and she put one on too. Then I had a top knot. My dark brown hair made my already porcelain skin look even whiter. I need a tan.

Squirrel

We blasted our favorite songs and went to Sonic for cherry limeades...I got half off! After that, we went to Lions Lake, that I love so much. I brought bread to feed the ducks and the one goose that stayed there. This was my ultimate way to chill and enjoy a beautiful day. We fed ducks for a bit, and I listened to her talk about her new man, Steve. She said he was really hot. He had brown hair and a stubble beard. He was tall. He was into most of the things she was into. She met him at the local university when they were having a career event. She went to check out the nursing program. He was there to look at their engineering program. He sounded amazing and I couldn't wait to meet him. She sounded head over heels for this cat! "He better be good to you." I said, "Or, Steve will have to answer for me!" She laughed, I laughed, we were having a blast. Then we hopped back in the car, and I took her home. We both had to work that night, and I could FINALLY drive myself!

At Sonic, I was a carhop. I took orders and made drinks, too. Mandi worked at Walmart. I wanted Mandi to work with me and Misty at Sonic because of the money and because it would be awesome working with her, but she said there was no way she'd be able to deal with my boss. She said she'd be fired on day one because she wouldn't take that crap and didn't know how I could. Sonic was awesome and really good money. We earned minimum wage plus tips, and sometimes I'd forget to pick up my paycheck because I earned so much money in tips that I didn't need my paycheck.

Best paying job ever for a teenager. We even had moms work there. Almost always the day shift, though. Sometimes, we'd get five or ten dollars from a customer! But it was usually a dollar or two, sometimes just change, but it all added up quickly, especially when you work over eight hours. We took our smoke breaks and meal breaks in the storage room. That was the only place. We would just have to find a box to sit on, and we would pay half the price for food to eat. If we got busy, our breaks would get cut short. Then we would get another one later. I wasn't a fan of my boss. He constantly yelled, cursed, and even threw sundaes we made…at us! But, like I said, it was very good money! My boss's name was Harry, which I have to laugh at, because he's bald. But, things were great when Harry was having a good day. He was funny and very considerate. So maybe he had bipolar disorder or just had mental issues. I have bipolar disorder, so that wasn't meant as a joke. If he were bipolar, it would all make sense. But he needed a medication adjustment if that was the case.

One Saturday, when I was off work, I decided to go for a drive and wondered how far 50 highway went. I hopped in my car and started driving. Man, I was flying, music was booming, and guys were checking me out. I was having the best time. Then I saw an exit for Chicago!! My friends from Arkansas and I dreamed of riding motorcycles one day to Chicago. So, I took the exit. I had to stop for gas, and little did I know, I was in Mount Olive, IL. I was about four hours from home. I decided I had better give my mom a call, but I couldn't remember if I even told her I left. When I called, she was crying and begging me to come home. So, I did. I was still flying high like nothing on the earth could touch me. It was insane but it was one of the best days of my life! Being manic is like nothing else. No drug can reproduce the feelings of being manic! However, it's not safe either. You don't think, you just act recklessly. And then there is always the depression that follows a manic episode. That's no fun at all.

That car ride to Illinois was my first manic episode. Then, I didn't know I had bipolar disorder. It wasn't bad. I was put on some mood stabilizers, and it seemed to take care of the problem dealing with my impulsiveness.

I still had a bit of a chip on my shoulder because we had just moved to Missouri from Arkansas, and I hated it! I missed all my friends in Arkansas. Little Rock wasn't a great area. My friends were into drugs, and then I started smoking marijuana and cigarettes. I even smoked it on our lunch breaks from school, and then went to school high. My dad took a tour to Korea for a year just to get us out of Little Rock. After doing a tour, my dad was allowed to pick a new base to move to. He decided to move us closer to my mom's family in Missouri. We moved to Warrensburg, close to the base, while waiting for a house. But I do have some great friends here in Missouri now. Some of them were older than me. Like out of high school. Heather and Dawn, to name a couple. They were in college, and I met Heather at Sonic, and Dawn at a college party.

I got along better with older girls, like 3 to 4 years older than me. Maybe it was a maturity thing except for Mandi. She was 17 and my best friend. And she wasn't immature in the least.

My sister, Michelle, and I were always best friends when we moved somewhere new, because we didn't have friends yet. But then we each made friends and returned to hating each other. We usually only stayed somewhere for 2 years, then we'd move again to another state…or country.

I was gothic I guess you could say. At least that's what I was told I looked like. Since my hair was very dark, and I wore a lot of dark colored clothes, heavy eyeliner, and sometimes dark lipstick. I guess that made me goth. I listened to a lot of heavy rock/metal, and alternative music. My parents hated that. I didn't take crap from anyone. I learned that in Arkansas.

One girl in my math class decided she had a problem with me and stood up in the middle of class like she was going to do something. So, I stood up. I'm thinking, *girl, I'm from Little Rock...bring it*. We just stared at each other, and the teacher told us to sit down. I was not sitting until this little wanna-be "bad girl" did. And, she finally sat down, *figures*, I thought. Then, I sat down. I just proved to the entire class not to mess with me.

After class, the teacher held me back. I was thinking, *why me and not that other girl?* As it turned out, she just wanted to say she knew that the other girl started it, that I've always been a good student, and that I was not in trouble. Cool I thought. I left to go to my next hated class. History. So boring! I had to work that night, too. I had so much homework and studying to do, as usual. And I seriously needed to hit the gym. I have been so busy that I haven't been able to go for a while. I need to make room in my schedule for it. Somehow. I worked to hard for this toned body to get flabby now!

Mandi and the girls asked if I was up for bowling that night. I told them, unfortunately, no. I had a ton of homework and had to study history, and I had to work. Mandi said she'd come over after school and she'd help me study. *Score*!! I thought. Mandi was hella smart, and I could use the help before I went to work. She came over, looking glamorous as always, and we hit the books. She quizzed me and threw me some curveball questions, but I got them right! We were done about an hour before I had to be at work. I thanked her and gave her a tight hug, and she left, then I got my uniform on for work.

I went by the bookstore that my mom worked at right before work. There was a car I had my eye on, sitting on the lot of one of the dealerships in town. It was a white cavalier! I had to find a way to get my mom on board to buy it. I got a book on cars off the bookshelf, it rates the cars and tells you the safety ratings, average mileage lifespan, etc. I found the Cavalier section in the book and wrote down everything on that car from the book. I studied there at the bookstore and researched the best and safest cars.

Before I went to work, I presented that to my mom and asked her if I could buy it. She said, "after doing all that research, how could I say no." Since I had to work, we were off to the dealer the next day, and I drove out of there with an awesome new car. My dad was still back in Korea. I missed him. But to be honest, I could get away with a lot more when he was gone. My mom was more chill. Like I said, I was home alone a lot.

I loved cleaning my car. It was always clean and detailed.

My new boyfriend, Tommy, whom I met through a mutual friend, was 21. He had a goatee and stood about 6 ft tall. He was attractive and really into me, which I liked, because I was really into him too. He programmed my car for me, the garage opener and hooked my stereo up. It wasn't the newest car on the market, so it needed some stuff installed. I just left all that to Tommy. It was too cool. I drove a Cavalier now! That is a huge upgrade from my grandma's old gold Impala with the seat heads still covered in plastic. He finished just in time for me to get to work. We said our goodbyes and shared a quick kiss, and off I went.

When I got to work, my boss, Harry, was on the rampage again. Screaming and hitting and kicking stuff. He screamed at me over nothing I did wrong, he just picked me. Then he grabbed a sundae and threw it at me.

That's it, I thought. *I didn't care about the money anymore, I'm quitting after this shift.*

But I didn't. I needed the money now to pay for my car, insurance, gas, and cell phone. But as soon as I'm in a better place financially, I'm done with this job. With this boss. I had had enough.

Tommy showed up at my work, as usual, but this time he had a necklace for me. He said, "Happy belated birthday." I really didn't have time to put it on, but he didn't really give me a choice. I leaned into his window, and he put it on me. It was a choker necklace that was brown and black beaded with a leather chain. It was just my style. I thanked him and told him I had to go, and we were swamped. He put in an order and requested I be his carhop.

But I did not see his order because another car hop took it. *Oh well*, I thought. Tommy was going to be pissed, though.

When we closed, I did my usual routine of cleaning all the machines and equipment, turning off the lights, and locking up. Then I drove my normal route home. When I got home, I locked the car doors before entering. Once inside I locked up, then went straight to the shower. Fast food really stinks. I washed uniforms every three days. I only had three uniforms, and I worked nearly every day. I undressed, dropped my clothes on the floor in the bathroom as usual, and hopped in the shower. It felt so good to get that grime and grease off me. It was so warm, and I felt like I could stay there forever. I even had my music playing on my phone. Perfect way to wind down after yet another crappy day at work. But at least Heather, Misty, and a few other friends were in the trenches with me. It made it tolerable and sometimes fun or at least as much fun as it could be.

Chapter 2: A Must Needed Break-up

After about six months, my dad was finally home! He brought us some really cool souvenirs from Korea. Perfumes, oils, blankets, and currency for me because he knows I collect them from all his travels. I have some currency from Saudi Arabia, too. I did miss him! He told us about his adventures in Korea and how he couldn't pick up their language, not even hello, in Korean. I laughed so hard. "What?" he said. "Nothing," I just laughed. He continued telling us that he was afraid to eat off the base because he heard they eat cats and dogs there. He said he thought about trying it but couldn't. "Good call." I said. The whole family laughed. He was really busy there, but we occasionally made calls over the computer with him.

He knew my boyfriend was 21 and he wasn't happy about it. We have been together about eight months now. My mom told him on a call when they were alone. I guess they just let it go because they thought I might rebel, and sooner or later, Tommy would probably get tired of not seeing me because of school and work, plus I couldn't go to bars with him, etc. Except they didn't know I had a fake ID, and that's exactly what I did.

During that eight-month period, Tommy became mentally abusive, almost physically, on a few occasions. The only one I told was Mandi. He was also becoming possessive.

I decided to break things off with Tommy. I didn't know how, but his possible reaction scared me. Besides being abusive, he turned out to be a major jerk and kind of psycho. I was avoiding him as much as I possibly could.

On my 17th birthday, he met me after work at my house and said he was taking me to a party. That wasn't what I wanted to be doing, but whatever, I guess. Mandi had to work that night anyway. So did Misty and Kaye. After cleaning up and on my way out the front door, my dad said, "Don't drink and drive." He says that every time my sister or I leave the house. But I know he means it and would pick me up in a heartbeat, and I wouldn't be in trouble.

This so-called "party" consisted of one other couple, plus Tommy and I. That was it. Four of us.

They were all high and drinking. Not me, though. I was so bored. There wasn't even any music playing. It was silent most the night. Or they'd be high and make a stupid joke that made no sense. I wanted to go home, but the jerk insisted on driving us there.

Happy birthday to me, I thought.

I wanted to be doing anything but this. Heck, I'd rather be at work. Maybe if it had been a rager party, with a large number of people, with lots of alcohol, it wouldn't be so bad, but it wasn't. Just the four of us, chilling, well, they were. My boredom turned to rage. I almost called my dad to pick me up, but I had no idea where we were, and Tommy would be pissed and probably wouldn't tell me. Maybe if he got drunk, I could tell him I was past curfew and I needed an address so my dad could get me. Eventually, they dialed down the drinking, but not the weed.

I snuck off to the bathroom, called my dad, and explained the situation. He said he knew where I was off the GPS on my phone when I selected "share location."

Thank God.

He said he was on his way and thanked me for calling him. I slipped out without Tommy even noticing. My dad was in their driveway, and I got in the car and my dad took me home. It was a quiet drive. I wasn't sure what to say. I did tell my dad about the weed, and that I didn't want to be around it, and thanked him for picking me up. He said, "Of course, I'm really glad you knew better and trusted me enough to call me. I'm sure that wasn't an easy decision."

When I got home, I called Mandi. It was late, but I had to vent to someone. She wished me a happy birthday and asked if I got her gift bag from my sister. She came by earlier, but I was at work. I told her no. I hadn't seen it anywhere. I asked my sister, Michelle, if she had it. She apologized as she forgot about it. She went into her room and got it. I opened the gift bag, and inside was the most beautiful crystal! I have loved collecting rocks and crystals since I was a kid. She knows me so well. It was an amethyst, too, which she knows is my favorite. I called her back and thanked her for her gift. It was so thoughtful. I can't wait for her birthday. I have the most awesome gift in mind!

That night Tommy called me, but I didn't answer. He called two more times. Then I decided to answer, otherwise he might come over.

"Where the hell are you?" he demanded. I told him I was home and getting ready for bed and that we could talk tomorrow.

"How the hell did you get home?" he asked.

"I said we can talk tomorrow," I repeated. Then I hung up.

The next day in his car, cruising around to show off his new speakers, I tried to talk to Tommy about my birthday, how upset I was that he didn't even ask me what I wanted to do, and the horrible time I had. He actually got pissed at me. I asked if he even noticed me gone. He said, "No." and took another puff off his cigarette. Well, that conversation went nowhere. He cranked up the stereo to cruise some more downtown. I asked him to turn it down and roll up the windows because I had a headache. He said just a little longer.

Um...no I thought. At the next stoplight, I got out of the car.

"What are you doing?" he yelled. "I said I have a headache," I answered. "You go cruising, I'm going home." He got pissed off again, then sped off to show off his new speakers.

I called Mandi and told her what happened, and she came and picked me up. "I can't believe what a prick he is," she said. I agreed. She dropped me off and I thanked her for the ride. She said, "You can thank me by breaking up with him." "Trust me, I'm getting there." I replied

He came to the house unexpectedly a few days later, and I didn't answer the door. I didn't want to see him. I was just lying on the couch. He wouldn't leave. I realized the curtains were open to the backyard, right in front of the couch. As I got up to shut them, I saw him coming around the back door. So, I laid back down and pretended to be sleeping.

So much for him thinking I'm not home.

He banged on the back door, but I just kept laying still. The next thing I knew, I heard him breaking into my bedroom window in the basement.

Holy crap, what is he doing I thought.

Then he came up the stairs and sat next to me. I pretended to be groggy from sleeping and asked him how he got in. He said I left the front door unlocked.

Bull Shit I said to myself.

He knows me better than that. I told him I locked the door, and he said he was worried about me, so he came in through my window. I told him I took some cold medicine and was asleep. I went downstairs to look at the window and he broke off a chunk of wood from the trim. Man, my dad is going to be pissed. He said he could fix it, and he tried, but he couldn't.

We were renting that house because we move so much. We either live on base or rent. I was pissed, and he knew it. Of course, he didn't care. He stayed there for another two hours, and I just wanted him to leave. We were watching music videos. He said he could tell me what any song was about that came on.

Really? I thought. *I think that's something most people can do.*

I finally told him I had to study so he needed to leave. He insisted on staying, and he would be quiet. So, I got my books out and started studying. *Man, this jerk can't take a hint.* I thought. I wanted him GONE.

He finally got bored and did leave. *Took long enough*, I thought. *Ugh, thank you, God.* What was I going to do about him?

Honestly, I was afraid to break up with Tommy. He was possessive and pretty much made it clear what I could do and could not do. It was getting worse. When he was there, some Jehovah's Witnesses came to my house, and I was very polite. He stood watching over my shoulder. When they left, he took the pamphlets they gave me and threw them in the trash, after ripping them to shreds. I wasn't planning to keep them, but that wasn't his place.

Another time around Christmas, my ex sent me a gift. It was a bottle of my favorite perfume. He was in the Air Force as well and stationed overseas. Before I had a chance to do anything with it, Tommy got pissed and grabbed it out of my hand and threw it in the trash. After he left, I dug it out. He would tell me things like, "I'd be his forever," and so on. Like total psycho talk. Like, he thinks he owns me, yea, I t think not. He wasn't even attractive to me anymore. He started to gross me out. I would squeal in my head when he kissed me. *YUCK*. I avoided kissing him as much as possible.

My friends kept telling me to break it off. Even my dad said to cut him loose. I said I wish I could, but he was like a stray evil cat, and kept coming back. I was trying my hardest to make HIM break up with me. I was just too scared.

Just last night I was hanging out with a new friend named Ashley. Tommy wanted a double date because his friend, Cline, who was single. Ashley agreed, but she quickly decided she wasn't interested. So, we told the guys we were going to steal a stop sign for my room. Ashley left her car at the fast-food place, and I drove us to my house for some tools. Then, we went down some country roads to find one. We found one, but we didn't have the right tools. We couldn't get it off. We left and went back into town. Then a car started flashing at me. It was Tommy. Ashley wanted to go home because she didn't like Cline and she was done for the night, but she didn't want them to know where she lived. I was so embarrassed about the whole situation. I doubt Ashley will want to hang out with me again. They followed and chased us through town, running red lights and all. What the hell was wrong with him?

We finally decided to go to the fast-food joint where she parked her car, and I would keep them busy so she could drive home. She got out of my car and into hers. She asked me if I was sure, and if I'd be ok. I told her I would and was so sorry about how tonight turned out. She said it wasn't my fault. She hugged me and left. Then Tommy approached me. He said I was so rude to Cline. He really liked Ashely. I told him she didn't like Cline, so we left. Then Cline got in his car and left, and I got into mine to return home.

I was backing out and suddenly saw Tommy in my rearview mirror. I got out. I said, "What are you doing? I almost hit you." Not a word. I told him to move out from behind me so I could leave. But he wouldn't move. Finally, he spoke. "Not until we talk," he said. I said, "I'm done talking, I'm tired and past curfew." I returned to my car and put it in reverse, and he still wouldn't move. I got out again and screamed at him to move. He just stood there with his arms crossed. I started screaming, "Somebody, please help me!" as loud as possible. There was a group of teens my age hanging out within earshot and about 15 of them. No one did anything.

I screamed again, "Somebody, please help me." Then four guys, probably a year older than me, started coming over, and one girl. When they got there, the guys just stood there next to me, and the girl said she would go in and get the manager and call the cops. I told her thank you so much. The guys stood with me, ready if Tommy tried anything. Finally, Tommy moved from behind my car and got in his car and left. I sat on the bumper of my car and started to cry. The guys comforted me, and said he was gone. I was safe to leave. I thanked them for protecting me, then I got in my car and left. I cried the whole way home. I prayed he wouldn't be there waiting for me. I texted my sister and asked her to look out front and see if he was there. She said I was all clear and it was time to break up with Tommy if I had to text her something like that. I told her I'd fill her in when I got home.

The next day, Tommy came over after I had left school. I had the courage and anger after what happened last night. I finally did it. I broke up with him. I told him he'd been acting like a total psycho, and it was over. He thought I was making a joke, but I'm pretty sure my eyes said it all. He knew I wasn't kidding. My mom and sister were home, so I felt safe. He left, and he was pissed. He peeled out of our neighborhood. *I'm glad that's over*, I thought.

He came over the next day, uninvited, as usual. *What? Did he think yesterday was just a bad dream?* I thought. I opened the door, but I wouldn't let him in. He tried to push past me, but I said he wasn't welcome inside. I came out and shut the door behind me. I told him that we were over. I told him I thought I made that pretty clear yesterday. I continued, I'm done with your mistreatment of me, and it's over. Then I asked him to leave, and I went back inside and shut and locked the door.

Whew...Did I really just do that? I thought.

I did! I was cheering in my head that I never had to talk to him, kiss him, or have anything to do with him again! He sat crying on my front doorstep for God knows how long. My dad came home from work and just stepped over him. *Are you kidding me?* I thought. My dad just stepped over him, crying like a baby. I thought to myself, be a man and leave! But it was finally over. He didn't seem scary to me anymore; he was more like an entitled crybaby.

Later, I would see him here and there at the bars, and then he would leave the establishment to avoid me. Why was I ever scared of him? I should have kicked him to the curb long ago, and I wished I had.

Chapter 3: School

The next night, Mandi, Misty, and I decided to go to Pine Street. Pine street was a magical place where the street was lined with multiple bars and dance clubs. Perfect for our college town! I love the dance clubs, and I was able to get a fake ID. My friends did as well, we got them through a guy at our school for about $20. You only had to be 19 to get in and 21 to drink. The bouncers didn't care if you had a fake ID or not. They would just hold the ID up to the camera, and they waved us in. We got our booze in the bathrooms from older friends who were always there. They would buy a round of beer, and we'd meet in the bathrooms and drink there.

I went to the actual bar for some water. After all the dancing, I was parched. When I was at the bar, this guy kept staring at me. He was sending some uncomfortable vibes. He asked me my name, and being polite, I told him it was Mac. He asked what kind of name that was, and I told him it was short for Makayla. He was hitting on me, and he was probably in his late 20s. I didn't find him attractive, so I wasn't up for flirting. I wanted to get back on the dance floor.

How long is this water going to take? I thought

I yelled to the bartender, "I'll be right back. I need to use the ladies' room." He waved at me, to acknowledge that he heard me.

After using the bathroom, I checked my make-up in the mirror, walked out, and saw that my water was on the counter where I had been standing. I was going to leave a tip on the bar, but I thought that weirdo might take it. I waved the bartender over with a few dollars in my hand. He came and got it and said thank you, then went back to making more drinks.

When I finished my water, I went back out to the dance floor to join my girls. All this dancing made me sweaty and thirsty. That guy from the bar kept staring at me. Suddenly, I started to feel bad. I hadn't had that much to drink, but I was getting foggy and felt like I was going to throw up. I raced to the ladies' room and did just that. When I came out, that guy from the bar was standing outside the ladies' room. He offered to help me and take me home; then he took me by the arm. His grip was so tight. I was so groggy, and I tried to pull away from him, I didn't know what was going on, but he was taking me to his car. I told him I had a ride. It fell on deaf ears. He said my friends had already left. I thought, no way, they wouldn't have left me, but he kept dragging me out of the bar.

Mandi and Misty saw the guy grabbing me by the arm and leading me out of the bar. They rushed over and stopped him and said they would take care of me and to let me go or they'd start screaming. So, he did. I rubbed my arm, it was throbbing because he was holding me so tight. They had to carry me out of there. Everything looked fake, I felt sick, and I was having a hard time talking and staying awake. Misty asked if I ever left my drink alone and I told her no, that we all drank in the bathroom...well, except my water, and I explained about going to the bathroom. What little I could remember anyway. They turned the car around and took me to the ER. There they took my blood, and sure enough, I was drugged. I had no idea who it was but suspected the guy from the bar since he was trying to take me home, or so he said. But I couldn't remember what he looked like, and I couldn't remember most of the night. I was glad my friends saw what was happening and got me out of there.

Sunday morning, I still wasn't feeling right. I obviously couldn't tell my parents why. They thought I was studying with Mandi and Misty at Mandi's house most of the night. I had to call into work. I told Harry that someone drugged me last night, and I couldn't come in. Silence. I started to tell him I had hospital papers to prove it, and he got pissed and said, "Well, nothing I can do about it," and he hung up on me.

Typical, I thought.

I woke up on Monday morning with the worst sore throat. My throat was scratchy and raw. My mom said I could stay home from school. It started to get worse as the day went on. My right ear was searing in pain. On Tuesday, I woke up exhausted from coughing all night, so I missed school again. My mom took me to the Dr. Wednesday morning, and I had pneumonia and strep throat. I must have picked it up while I was in the hospital. Which reminded me,

I was going to have to fess up that I wasn't studying and Mandi's that night and that I was at a bar and got drugged and was seen at the hospital because there was sure to be a bill in the mail.

When we got home, I figured I might as well just tell her. "Mom", I said, then I told her the whole story. She said she was very upset, and I was grounded, and then she started crying. She told me she was so glad my friends saw what was going on. "And by the way," she said. "How did you girls even get into the bar?" I was not about to fess up my fake ID, so I told her that Misty's brother was working at the door checking IDs, and he let us in. But we just went to dance. She was not happy. She told me to NEVER leave a drink unattended, not for one second. She said, "If you turn to talk to someone, your water should be in your hand facing them; never turn your head from your drink." "Trust me, Mom." I said, "I learned my lesson."

I ended up missing that entire week of school and work from being sick. The pneumonia was kicking my butt. They ended up having to give me shots in my hip and breathing treatments.

I figured Harry was probably going to fire me. Then again, I was one of his best employees, so I doubt it. Over the weekend I finally started feeling better. On Monday, I was able to go back to school. I still wasn't feeling well but I had a TON of makeup work to do, and I had to work the next four nights at Sonic too.

All but one of my teachers were great about catching me up and getting me my missed assignments. The exception was my Chemistry teacher. I went to Chemistry and my teacher handed me a test and told me to go to the empty classroom across from us to take it. The test covered everything they went over the week I was sick. She said to just use my partner's notes, and sent me to another room. I had a doctor's note, so this was totally unfair.

I walked across the hallway to the empty classroom, then sat down and looked over the test and my partner's notes. I couldn't answer a single question. My 'partners' notes were a total joke. They didn't help me out at all. I returned to class and asked if I could take it after finishing my make-up work. I couldn't answer a single question. She said, "Well, I guess you'll take an F then." I reminded her of my missed week of school due to excused absence, with a doctor's note, but it fell on deaf ears. So, I calmly returned to my desk, returned my partner's notes, gathered my things, and left. Like, left left. I went home and didn't tell anyone. I had had enough that day, and I was feeling out of control with my temper, and I should probably tell my psychiatrist about that. I don't know if it was a bipolar thing or not. I hadn't slept for two days because of the insomnia or possible mania that hit me too over the weekend.

Shortly after I arrived home, the phone rang.

Do I answer it? I thought.

I hesitantly answered, "Hello," I said. It was my principal calling me. I explained what happened, and he said he understood, and if I had just come to him, I wouldn't be in trouble. But I wasn't thinking. I was just acting impulsively. He asked me if I was having a manic episode, and I told him I didn't think so. And if I was, would I still be in trouble? He laughed, "Yea," he said, "You'd still be in trouble".

Yea, definitely some mania going on, as I thought about my behavior.

My principal was awesome. He always had my back, but even though he liked me a lot and I was one of his favorites, I was still in trouble for walking out of class and school. But his hands were tied so I received a three-day, in-school suspension for walking out of class and driving myself home.

In-school suspension was horrible. I fell asleep for the first time in days but the detention teacher rudely woke me up. Boy was I hot! And sleep-deprived.

Maybe my meds do need to be adjusted, I thought.

After the third night without sleep, my mom had me lie down, then she laid behind me and played with my hair and rubbed my back. And what do you know…baam…out like a light! After I woke up, I felt so much better. It was like the best power nap!

My Spanish teacher was a witch, too. After I asked a question in class, she openly said in front of the whole class, "you don't need to ask any more questions, Mac, you aren't passing this class regardless."

I couldn't believe she just announced that in front of the whole class. Some students were even laughing. So, I started working on Chemistry which I was also about to flunk. Then she told me I couldn't. That made no sense to me. Not to mention she had already embarrassed the crap out of me. So I said, "Well, since you have already established to the entire class that I'm not passing your class, I have other classes to work on." She still made me put my book away.

I'm so done with school, I thought.

Spanish was my last class, so I told the principal what my Spanish teacher did in class. He said he'd take care of it. He asked me if I was having problems with any other teachers. I told him that another one of my teachers wasn't letting me take my 'State of Missouri' test because I missed my last test. I need a passing grade on that test to graduate. But I missed my test day because that was when I was sick and I had a doctor's note, but he still wouldn't schedule a time for me to take it. That made no sense to me. He asked if I had time now, so I told him yes. Then we walked down to his class, and he showed my teacher the doctor's note, and he told him to administer the test to me right away.

Ohhhh, someone is in trouble, I said to myself. I couldn't help but smile.

The teacher shot me a dirty look, and I just smiled again. I took the test and went home.

I hated my high school so much that I told my counselor that if I couldn't go to college for dual credit, I would drop out of high school. I couldn't stand the two mean teachers I had, and I was tired of being treated like a child. The counselor called my mom at work, and she was able to get away for about an hour. When she got there, we all sat down to figure out what to do. He said I could go to the local university, and be on the college campus and get dual credit for my high school classes, but if I failed one class, I wouldn't graduate. I thought about that momentarily and told him, "Let's do it." I was a senior anyway, and dual credit was common, so now they would let me as a second-semester senior get dual credit also because my IQ and prep ACT and SAT scores were so high.

Basically, I went to high school for my internships and then the college campus. I loved the college atmosphere and all my classes. The atmosphere and not being treated like a child was a huge change.

I met my new boyfriend, Jaden, at a college frat party. Dawn and I were on our way upstairs, and he was going downstairs in the frat house. We locked eyes, and he stopped, almost knocking his buddy down the stairs. It was a mutual instant attraction. He was very easy on the eyes. He was clean-shaven, tall, with dark brown hair, and oh-so muscular. His eyes were ice blue. He told me he would be returning with more beer, and he asked me if I'd be here when he got back.

"Sure, I'll see you in a bit," I answered him in a seductive yet innocent voice, with a half-smile. I'd wait for him, I couldn't wait until he got back. He said he'd come find me when he got back.

About thirty minutes later, he came back, and I heard he was frantically looking for me. He thought maybe I left. I was told he was going from room to room looking for me. I was going to stand in the hall so he could find me, but then he came in the room I was drinking in. Then we went into the hallway, and he asked my name.

I said, "My name is Makayla, but everyone calls me Mac. What is your name?"

"Jaden," he said.

I told him he had a cool name, he said Mac was a cool name, too. I told him it was nice to meet him. He said, "Follow me." I told Dawn I was going with him, and she said, "have fun!"

He gave me a tour of the frat house. They had trash bag slip and slides in the hallways, more solo cups than I have ever seen, and multiple kegs. It was crazy! I was having a blast! I was getting drunk and started making out with Jaden.

"You are the best kisser," he said. "You aren't too bad yourself," I responded. We stayed together all night. I just couldn't shake it. I was at a frat party with the hottest guy there! Their parties were amazing to say the least. We had so much fun together. We became boyfriend and girlfriend right away. It was crazy and moved so fast.

One night, I snuck out and went to one of their parties. It was a total rager! I got drunk. I drank some water, and he got me something to eat so I could drive home. Finally, about an hour later, I started to sober up. I only lived about five minutes away. So, I left, reached home, quietly walked in and went straight to my room. I got my pajamas on and went upstairs to get some water. I went to the sink and looked out the window over the sink. There was a man under the streetlight. He was wearing a hoodie with the hood over his ballcap. He was leaning up against his car and looking at my house. I couldn't make out his face, but the car was a grayish blue, maybe, and there was a dent on the back right fender. I shut the lights off as fast as I could and checked that the door was locked, then went to the basement where my room was.

Maybe he was just waiting on one of my neighbors. Of course, I couldn't tell my parents the next day because it was 3 a.m. and I had snuck out. It was so unnerving!

Who is that guy, and what was he doing out there? I shook it off and went to bed.

With my room in the basement, there weren't any closets or anything, so my mom got me some standing closets to hang my clothes on. The basement was awesome because it was way more spacious than my room and I had more privacy. I had my bed, a sitting area with couches, a TV, and speakers for my music. That night I slept with one of the big kitchen knives under my pillow! I was still freaked out by what I saw outside the window.

The next day, before I had to be at work, I went to see Jaden and hung out for a bit. Well, let's say that I walked in on him watching Teletubbies. If you don't know what that is, it's a wordless show with stuffed characters that just made noises. It's probably like its intended audience...children who can't speak yet. Not a college frat boy. We had been together for a few months. I was starting to think I needed to break things off. I mean, I love parties and all, but not every night. I had ambitions, I wasn't sure Jaden did. He was probably high again. I sat there for a bit and decided I needed to go and study. This was a waste of my time. He begged me to stay, but I told him I had to study before work, and I left. I really thought about breaking things off with him. I needed more out of a "man." Looks will only get you so far.

Shockingly, the next night, out of the blue, he asked if he could take me to dinner. We always went halves, but he said the sweetest thing to me. He said, "You work so hard and study your ass off, and I just get money whenever I want it, so I want to treat you."

Oh wow, this was a new Jaden! Could he tell I was about to dump him? We went out to the local Applebee's and I got their crispy chicken and honey mustard salad, and he got a steak. The meal was amazing. He paid for everything this time. I thanked him again. Then I drove us back to the fraternity. I stayed another hour or so, and we made out and talked about what we were going to do after college. I was going to be in the FBI, God willing, and he was going to go corporate. I told him I wanted to be a profiler or field agent.

He didn't have a car, which I found odd, so I drove. He gave me a rose once when I was picking him up and I thought it was so sweet. He was really stepping up. Maybe he really did think he was about to lose me, and he was. I could see the effort he was putting in, but it wasn't enough.

I picked him up to go to a party, then I found out he had marijuana in my car. I'm a Criminal Justice major, so that would not have looked good if I had gotten caught with that in my car. I was pissed. After I dropped him back off, I threw that stupid rose out the window. I was hoping he'd see it in the parking lot, so he would know how much he just screwed up.

The next day, I picked up another job because school was getting expensive. I found one at a clothing store in town. More like a boutique. I worked eight-hours at Sonic, raced home and showered, then went to work four hours at the clothing store, and closed several evenings a week. That was a 12-hour workday. I decided I wanted some dinner before studying. Since I was home alone, I hopped in my car and started driving to Burger King.

I looked in my rearview mirror, and oh my gosh! That car with the dent in the fender was two cars behind me. It had to be a coincidence. I looked in my rearview at the perfect moment and saw it in the streetlight. Was this guy following me, or was this just a fluke? About three hundred and forty-eight thousand alarm bells were going off in my head. I took a couple of turns to see if he stayed behind me.

What do I do? I asked myself.

I decided to drive to the police station. Once I pulled in, he continued driving straight.

Whew!

That was a crazy coincidence, or some guy was following me around. I called Mandi and told her about sneaking out and then she told me to file a report. But I didn't feel I had enough to file anything. It's not like the guy was stalking me or anything…or was he?

Chapter 4: I'm Being Stalked

After I got home from Burger King, I went down my room. I was in shock and couldn't believe what I was seeing. Those three hundred and forty-eight thousand alarm bells were going off again in my head. Both my closets were tipped over, and my clothes were a wreck!

How on earth did they fall over? In over a year, this has never happened. Maybe the cat? I don't know. I found those straps that came with them to attach them to the wall, and I installed them. Well, I thought, this won't happen again! After I got all of them set up again, I started hanging the hangers back up with my clothes on them. Still curious how they all fell over.

When I finished, I went upstairs for a pudding pop, my favorite. I went back to my room and started drawing, more like sketching so I could paint over my drawing. I did abstract painting because I couldn't paint anything real. I was trying to learn how to, but I seriously sucked at it. Unfortunately, my sketching also sucked. Forget it, I decided. I took a few pages of alcohol ink paper to my drafting table. I plugged in the machine made to spray paint, but in my case, I used it to spray air. I made the most beautiful purple flower. It looks a lot like watercolor, but it's more bold. I was so proud of it I ended up framing it. I tried a few more flowers, but they weren't as good as my first one. I went and got a blank canvas and started making abstract art. I used squares this time with acrylic paint. No size or color pattern, just making random squares with random colors until the canvas was covered.

Perfect! I thought to myself.

I like this one, but need to find somewhere to hang it. I figured I'd better get some studying done. My homework was done, but had a test coming up. I studied for about an hour, then I got tired. It was late so I decided to turn in for the night.

That night, or the following day technically, my alarm started blaring at three am!

What the hell?

My alarm is always set to go off at six am! I wondered if the guy I saw outside my house did this and knocked over my closets.

Do I have a stalker? I had a thought.

Why did he set it for three am? Is he outside my house again? The last time I actually saw him was when he was leaning up against his car, and it was three am. I left all the lights off and slowly moved to the kitchen. It was dark. I peeked out the window, and sure enough, he was there. Leaning on his car under the streetlight.

Crap! What do I do?

I left my phone downstairs, so, I woke up my mom and told her to call the cops. That he was outside the house, she got up to look, and he was gone.

Damn it, I screamed in my head.

"Mac, it's early, I think you are just seeing things."

Seriously?

I told my mom about my alarm, but she obviously just wanted to go back to bed. So, I just stopped and went back downstairs to my room. I set my alarm to six am again, but I couldn't fall back to sleep.

The next day I was exhausted. I was still working two jobs, both Sonic and a clothing store. I also had an internship with the District Attorney's office. I loved working with the District Attorney. I got to go to court and sit up front with her while she did her cases. I handed her the folders she needed, took notes, etc. Working at the DA's office really cemented my desire to be in law enforcement. I knew for sure that I wanted to be an FBI agent. One of my professors at the college was a retired profiler for the FBI, and he told us lots of stories. It was then solid in my heart that I was going to be in the FBI. Period.

I told the DA about my situation with this random guy, both at my house and following me. She said she would have the police drive around my neighborhood here and there. They had a description of the vehicle. She said they usually don't patrol in my area because we were on the outskirts of town, but she would talk to the police commissioner and plead my case. Maybe a police presence would scare off this guy. I thanked her very much.

I asked her if this was indeed someone stalking me. She said, "Yes." She told me about the laws regarding stalkers. I wish I knew who he was, then this would be over, I would think. The cops could arrest him, and I'd happily press charges and get a restraining order in the meantime…but I doubt he would even obey the restraining order. I'd probably make him even more mad.

After my internship concluded for the day, I needed to head to campus. I noticed my car door was unlocked.

Weird.

I checked the back seats, then got in my car and turned the key. To my surprise my battery was dead, and the headlights were on.

What?

I didn't even use my headlights. All the doors were unlocked. That is not even fathomable. With OCD and being stalked, ALL my doors are always locked. It was him. It had to be. I walked back into the DA's office to call my mom since my cell phone was dead too. I told her I needed her to come jump my car. She replied she was on her way.

A police officer, Officer John, was there. He said he'd jump it for me. I quickly called my mom back and told her I was good. Luckily, she hadn't left work yet. I thanked him and told him that I needed to file a report. I told him about, I guess I can say it now, my stalker. As soon as I mentioned I had a stalker, his ears perked up. He called the station and got put in the circle of people to look out for me. He walked me back to my car from the building. My car was good to go, and he watched me drive off.

Crap.

I'm going to be late for class, and they lock the doors when you are late. This was getting ridiculous. I was pretty shaken, but I just remembered he is too chicken to show himself, at least not yet. For now, I'm fine, and I have a life to live. Since my class on campus was bound to be locked, I decided I needed some calming tea. I went to this cute little cafe on campus and got some. I sat there and studied until my next class, sipping my tea.

A few weeks had passed, and I left another eight hour shift at Sonic. I noticed the bluish-gray car following me around town again. This time, it was closer. He wasn't two to three cars behind me as usual, but right behind me. I was getting used to it, or maybe more like it wasn't a shock to me anymore. I was just waiting for him to get bored and move on, but this wasn't his norm, whoever he was. This time, he was following so closely that he hit me! I went straight to the police station, but there was no paint from his car on my bumper.

Dang it!

It freaked me out, but then again, he never approached me. Why? He was escalating. I bought a huge knife, right at the law's allowance, to carry around before I got home.

When I got home, I was adding all my tips, that's when I came across a five-dollar bill. It had written on it, in blood red ink, "It was great seeing you up close." That couldn't be a coincidence. I flipped the bill over, and it said, "See you again soon."

Yep, that sealed it, it was him!

I was freaked out but happy. I had a handwriting sample and possibly a fingerprint. I immediately put the bill in a zip lock bag, and took the bill to the police officer I was working with, Officer John, or Johnny, as he said I could call him, but I kept calling him Officer John. He said they'd do their best, but it was nearly impossible to find out who it was with the money because there were tons of fingerprints on it.

Duh, I thought to myself.

Of course there is. I should have known that. But Officer John warned me, he was escalating, which I knew. I didn't feel so happy anymore. I just wanted this jerk to leave me alone. To quit being a scaredy cat and show his face to me! Why me? What did I do? Where did he first see me, and why did he start stalking me? They kept the bill for evidence, so when they finally caught him, they had that as evidence in court. Officer John offered me five dollars from his wallet since they kept mine for evidence. You know, poor college kids and all.

He said, "You are a hard-working college student, get some coffee with it."

I politely declined but told him that was so sweet of him. He insisted, so I took it and thanked him.

Officer John was the coolest. I felt so much better knowing he was specifically assigned to me. He gave me his cell phone number, so I could just call his cell if I needed anything. It would get to him faster. If for some reason, he didn't answer, he asked to leave a message and call the station, especially if it was urgent. This way someone else would be there quickly until he got my message. I thanked him and assured him I'd do that. He reminded me that he was the head of my case, so not to hesitate to call him if ANYTHING happened, or if something felt off. I thanked him again and headed home.

Later that night, I found out my dad was leaving for Korea again, and then he would be in Saudi Arabia for a few months. I was so bummed. He's never been on this many deployments before. It's like he was never home. I missed him while he was gone, especially now with the stalker on the loose. I'm losing a male presence.

That next evening, we all said our goodbyes, and off he went with very little luggage. He always brought an extra empty luggage bag with him for the souvenirs he got for us.

I forgot my biology textbook at Mandi's, so I headed there to grab it. I told her my dad was leaving again. This deployment was six months to a year. She gave me a big hug as I teared up.

"It just feels safer when he's home," I cried.

She gave me another big hug and said everything would be ok. I had the police making rounds, I had a couple of weapons, and my mom was still there, even though she worked a lot. But she reminded me I'm rarely home alone. And if I ever felt uneasy, I could always come to her house. I cried again and hugged her. "Thank you for being the best bestie on the planet."

She said, "I know I am, so don't you forget it".

We both laughed. I gave her another hug, and then I headed home.

My mind was flooded. I wasn't sure if I would ever get the answers to my questions. I've never had a conversation with the stalker, at least that I know of. What he wrote on the $5 bill was so eerie. I cannot believe I was that close to him and didn't know it. We were so busy I must not have noticed his car, or he drove another one I haven't seen. I just wanted to scream at him to leave me alone! He obviously wanted me scared and stuck in my home, but I wasn't going to allow the psycho to dictate my life and what I could and could not do. Especially because I'm halfway to being 18-years-old and an adult! Not that it means anything in stalker land, but it did to me.

Officer John went to my mom's work to let her know that I was carrying around a knife because he didn't want me to. He said that my stalker could easily turn the knife on me. He also had a patrol car drive around our neighborhood occasionally, hoping that a police presence might scare him off, even though the DA already requested that. But it did not scare him off, and he was still stalking me.

Officer John told me that this would end with a physical altercation, possibly rape, an abduction, or possibly killing me. That is how these types of stalking usually end. That scared the crap out of me. I was scared of how this could end, but I was also getting myself ready for that inevitable confrontation. However, I kind of felt empowered, and I could take care of myself, why? No idea, after all, I was only a 17-year-old girl. But I was in shape and felt like I could take on anyone. I had a knife and pepper spray and never went anywhere without them. Even around the house

I just finished another grueling shift at Sonic. When I got home and realized I had forgotten my new keys to the house since we had changed the locks. I went to the garage door and pulled the handle on the bottom as hard as possible, and it opened right up!

Score!

I desperately needed a long, hot shower after today's shift. Harry wasn't "too" bad today, so that was a win, but tonight I had to cook, make drinks, and car hop. We were short-staffed. The front door was locked, so I went into the bathroom and locked the door. I undressed and hopped in the shower. It felt so good. I started singing like I always do when no one is home. I was squeaky clean. I opened the curtains and grabbed my towel and wrapped it snugly around me. I opened the bathroom door, and I felt a breeze. I decided to investigate, and walked out of the bathroom and around the corner to the living room where I felt the breeze coming from. I looked in the living room in sheer terror!

Chapter 5: He's Escalating

The furniture in the living room was moved around, the back door was wide open with my dad's grill pushed in front of it, and when I went to close it, I froze in terror when I saw it. My heart was pounding in my chest, with my mouth gaping open.

My work clothes were in the middle of the living room, piled on the floor. I hadn't even noticed when I got out of the shower that my clothes were missing or that I didn't have to unlock the door until now! Was he still here?

Moments later, my sister and a few of her friends came through the door laughing. Oh, it was them! I started screaming at my sister that this shit wasn't funny, not in the least. They all got quiet. My sister, Michelle, said, "Mac, seriously, I just got home. What happened?"

"Look," I told her, holding up my uniform.

"He was in the bathroom while I was in the shower, he moved all this around. And my work clothes were in the middle of the floor! So, he came in the bathroom while I was taking a shower," I screamed.

Michelle ran her hands through her blonde hair like she didn't know what to think. She asked if I called the police. I said no, I just got out of the shower and saw all this, and then you came home. I asked Michelle if she or her friends saw anything outside on their way here, but they all said no.

I called Officer John since I had his cell phone number, and I told him what had happened. He said he was on his way. I told Michelle and her friends not to touch anything. Then I went downstairs, cautiously, to get dressed. Michelle went with me, and I had pepper spray in hand just in case he was waiting for me. No one was down there, so Michelle went back upstairs. She quickly explained to her friends that I had a stalker because they didn't know what was happening.

About 15 minutes later, I heard sirens, and Officer John was on my doorstep. I left everything as it was, except I shut and locked the back door. He asked if I touched anything else and I said that I picked up my work clothes, but I put them back to where they were. Other officers were taking pictures and dusting for fingerprints on the bathroom door, the sliding back door, and pretty much anything he could have touched. They were dusted with some kind of powder and lifting prints using special tape. They also used a sticky roller to try and find hairs. Officer John said my mom was on her way from work and told me not to panic. How could I not panic? This psycho was in the bathroom while I was in the shower, helpless and naked.

The other officers were questioning my sister and her friends. Then, we all had to give our fingerprints to rule out the crime scene prints. It was like the movies.

"Mac, Mac!" I suddenly heard Officer John calling my name.

"Are you ok?" he asked

Before I could answer, he said, "Sorry, dumb question." And I grinned.

He smiled, "I don't want to scare you more than you probably already are, but your stalker is escalating. Mac, do your best not to be alone, check your back seats before getting into your car, consider moving your room back upstairs where there are fewer places to hide, things like that."

I nodded, but I was still in shock. I couldn't get over it. I was in the shower when he came in and took my clothes. Naked. Singing away, so I didn't hear him. Though I'm glad I didn't hear him. What if I looked out from the curtains, and saw him, and he saw me? Maybe he would have attacked me right then. I just couldn't get it out of my mind. It kept circling in my mind nonstop. HE WAS IN THE BATHROOM WHILE I WAS NAKED IN THE SHOWER! He wanted to let me know he could get to me anywhere. And he proved that.

I just prayed that they would find something that could end this. I'm not sure what charges could be brought, but from what I researched, "Stalking Is now a prohibited act in the law of every state. It is defined as the intentionally repeated following of a person to harass the person with expressed or implied threats of violence or death, their main goal was for the victim to acknowledge them."

He has been acknowledged! So why is he still stalking me?

I researched and read that "there are four types of stalkers: surveillance, life invasion, intimidation, and interference through sabotage or attack. I felt like he was hitting all four categories. I didn't have much support at the beginning of all of this, but now no one can deny I'm being stalked in a significant way. The outlook was not looking good. Stalkers are likely to be very intelligent and organized, have a huge ego, and a need to control their victims. They like to play games, like a cat toying with a mouse. He researches his victims thoroughly, picks them, studies them, and learns everything about them before he moves. Likely a sociopath," I read.

Once, my sister had her boyfriend, and his friends hide in the bushes when I came home from work. They had baseball bats ready to go when his car showed up, which it didn't. He never followed me all the way home. He is well aware I know that he knows where I live. He didn't need to prove that anymore... but that was very sweet of them to do that for me.

Summer was approaching quickly, and I was really looking forward to working at the lake with my friends, and getting a break from this freak! The lake was about three hours away, and I was hoping that it would end the stalking without confrontation. We kept our plans on the "down low," so it wouldn't somehow get back to my stalker.

Driving to the lake, I will need to check my rearview mirror constantly. Put very simply, I was excited to be on my own and free of this stalker. I wanted to know who he was, but not enough to actually be close enough to him to see.

This was really getting me panicked. Panicked to do anything. I didn't feel safe at home. He stalked me more at my home than outside the house. I thought of how this could end, trying to figure out how I would survive with all the "what if" scenarios going on in my mind until I fell asleep. And falling asleep took a while.

Before my class started, I decided to talk to my professor, Professor Wilson, who was a former FBI profiler. His office hours were open right now. I told him everything, and I asked for his thoughts.

He said, "It sounds like the police have you well covered." He continued, "I agree that this type of stalking is not going to end well, Mac."

I started to cry. He said he had no idea I was going through all this and that I am a powerful woman. "Despite all this," he said, "you have the highest grade in my class. All my classes, actually."

That made me smile a little. "Your stalker is obsessed with you and wants you to notice him. He wants to know everything about you. He thinks he loves you, and he wants your attention. He's jealous of anyone who takes your attention, and he escalates. He's probably in your everyday life. However, I think he is probably in his late 20s," he continued, "I would suggest you take some self-defense classes and keep your pepper spray on you at all times. Get a better security system with cameras that will give you a notification on your phone and keep your phone on you at all times. If you have pants that don't have pockets for your phone, don't wear them. With this type of system, anyone who approaches your home, whether the alarm is armed or not, it will notify you."

"I hope my parents can afford that," I said.

"I have a feeling they will find a way to afford it. You are their daughter, and this is serious." he replied.

"These systems even record events so you can look at them later. The images are clear, and they have night vision too. But getting that notice that someone is approaching your house could be the very thing that saves you. You can call the police, get your pepper spray, and hide somewhere until the cops show up. Hide somewhere you can lock yourself in if you can. I would also get a doorknob for your bathroom that requires a key. It's not a lifesaver, kicking down an interior door is not hard to do, but it's a deterrent."

"Thank you so much, Sir," I said. "Can you write down the name of this security system so I can give it to my mom? Unfortunately, my dad is deployed right now."

He said sure and wrote it down. "Here is my card, in case you have more questions, or your mom does." "Thank you so much," I said. "I'll see you tomorrow in class." After our discussion, I left to attend the rest of my classes. I couldn't concentrate at all. I missed so many notes, and tests were coming up.

Ugh, I need to concentrate, I told myself.

After my classes, I stopped by Jaden's fraternity house on the way to say hello and hang out for a little bit. I told him what happened, and he didn't seem to care. I think he was high. Jaden was watching music videos. I was baffled that he didn't care about this freak stalking his "girlfriend" or that I was scared for my life!

I left, and he was upset, and I was upset too. I had things to do, I just needed to get home to study. He was just a rich boy on a free ride in college, thanks to mommy and daddy. I was starting to think again that we should be over. He wasn't quite what I thought he was in the beginning. But that sealed it. He isn't for me. I'm too type A and an overachiever, and I don't sit around all day watching whatever is on TV. I needed to be around people who were succeeding. To keep my spirits up and keep me going. I like to grow. I like to be around successful people. I mean, straight A's in your first year of college is pretty good.

I was supposed to meet up with Jaden for dinner, but he said he was so sorry, and needed to visit his parents out of town. I told him to have a safe drive, and we would get together when he returned. I think I'll break things off when he gets back.

Later that evening I passed the fraternity house on the way to grab a bite to eat. I saw Dawn's car, and I suspected that Jaden was still there. I wanted to go in, and I had an excuse. I made cookies for all the guys and left my mom's plate there. Hmmm, I thought. I guess I could go in and get it. Dawn never went to the frat house without me, and we would always see Jaden and his friends. She was a slut. I'll just be blunt. And she was getting a reputation and fast. Just about every time we went there, she was sleeping with one of the frat guys. I told her she was getting a bad reputation, but she said she didn't care.

I turned my car around and went into the frat house. I headed straight to Jaden's room. A few guys tried to distract me I could tell. The others were probably telling Jaden I was there. But I pushed past them and kept walking. I got to Jaden's room, but the door was closed. That wasn't normal. I opened the door without knocking, it was unlocked. I flipped on the lights; I saw it with my own eyes. Jaden was on the top bunk naked, having sex with some girl I later learned was his ex, and Dawn was on the bottom bunk with one of the frat brothers named Eric, and they were also having sex.

Gross, I thought. *Couldn't they use separate rooms?*

"Out of town to see your parents, huh? What, you can't be a real man and just break things off?" I asked him.

He was so drunk and high he told me it was not what It looked like, and he still loved me. He was just drunk and made a mistake. Then SLAP! His ex slapped him across the face and started getting dressed. Then Jaden stumbled to get his pants on and climb down the bunk bed. He came up to me and begged me to hear him out. I slapped him as hard as I could.

"We are over if that's not obvious now," I told him. "Don't call me, text me, in fact, just stay far away from me. When you see me on campus, go the other way. We are over." I yelled at him.

I saw my mom's plate, and I grabbed it. "Good luck, girl, with him," I said.

Then I looked at Dawn. She had a shocked expression on her face. Her short, dirty blond hair was all messy from sex. I decided I was done with her. I said, "As for you, my so-called friend, lose my number. I want nothing to do with you anymore, got it?"

"Enough already with both of you. Enjoy your evening." I said, and I slammed the door behind me. All the frat guys in the hallway were dead silent. Except one brave soul. He said, "I'm so sorry, Mac. Jaden's an ass."

I told him I agreed one hundred percent. Then I stormed out of there and went home. I was really hurt that he lied to me and cheated on me, but I'm glad I caught him in the act. It's just another reason to break up with him. And Dawn, a reason to quit being friends with her. I didn't want the reputation she has. A total slut.

Dawn called me the following day, and I didn't want to answer, but I did. She wanted to know why I dumped her as a friend. She said she was going to call me tomorrow and tell me Jaden cheated on me. I told her I didn't have time for part-time friendships, especially those who betray me, while dealing with a stalker, school, work, etc. I told her she was acting like a slut. And I wasn't like that. Like when she told me that "In college, you sleep around, it's called being a grown-up." Yes, she actually said that. "I couldn't believe you actually said that to me." I told her what happened last night was just the straw that broke the camel's back. Then I said I meant what I said, "lose my number." Then I hung up on her.

Ugh, the nerve of that girl!

Later that week, at the gas station, I ran into some of Jaden's frat brothers who told me how stupid Jaden was because I was "the whole package." Then, one of them actually asked me out. I toyed with it for a minute, that would make Jaden crazy. Ha, So funny! But not worth it. I don't have the emotions to get played again by some frat guy. I am having a hard enough time dealing with a stalker from hell, I don't need the stress. "I appreciate you asking me out, but I've decided to stay single for awhile." I told him.

When my mom got home from work, I told her about what my professor had said and gave her the slip of paper with the security system information. She said she'd look it over, and next time she talked to dad, they would discuss who would be best to get it from. I told her thank you and that she would get the notifications, too. They would all be on an app we downloaded. *Oh, crap,* I thought. No more sneaking out. Well, I might be able to find a way around it!

I decided that I was going to take self-defense classes. I found a place in town that taught Jujitsu, and it was affordable. They also had discounts for college students. I worked really hard. I was able to flip over a 250 pound man. I learned how to break away from someone, I learned how to put them in a chokehold, I learned how to break fingers around my neck or anywhere else. Let's say I learned a lot, and he had to have known it. With all his following, I'm sure he saw me go in there. Maybe that would be a reason for him to back off some.

My instructor's name was Levi, and he was amazing. I told him why I was taking the classes, so he tailored some different moves for me while the class did others. There were typically two to three instructors there, so it wasn't a big deal. He was very handsome, OK, I know I use the word a lot, but he was hot!! He was about an inch shorter than me, dark brown hair, clean-shaven, and had the most gorgeous big brown eyes. His chin was chiseled, and he had a lot of strength but not super muscular. He was just right. I would never dare tell him that, though, or he might drop me as a student. Heck, he probably had a girlfriend. After class I thanked him so much for taking the time again to work with me solo. Then I drove home to grab a shower and head to bed.

I woke up the next morning without the creep on my mind. It felt good! I played some music and danced around the house because I was home alone. I threw in some laundry and decided to see Mandi since days without much to do were rare. I was seriously way too busy most days and I needed, I wanted, to make sure I had time for her. The lake will come soon! I hadn't even told her about half the stuff going on yet. I wanted to tell her in person and not on the phone. I needed support and someone to listen to my worries. I didn't want to talk about it today because I felt so good, but I needed to.

On my way to Mandi's house, I saw he was following me again.

Damn it, I screamed in my head.

He followed me almost daily at this point. My house being messed with didn't even come to mind with this car following me around. I got to Mandi's house and kept driving, then pulled into a random house's driveway. He was still behind me when I turned into the driveway, but he kept going. Then I pulled out and called Mandi. She told me she'd open the garage, and I could park in there so he couldn't see my car. At this point, I was scared all the time. The Jiujitsu classes were helping a lot, and I always had my knife and pepper spray out and ready to go.

I hung out with Mandi for a couple of hours. She is always so supportive and knows exactly what to say. I heard more about her new man, Steve, that she's dating. I saw a selfie she took with the two of them…he was a looker! I said, "Go girl!" In the picture, he had brown hair and was extremely fit. He had gorgeous eyes and was tall. After we shared some of what was happening and got caught up, I headed home. I had an exam the next day and needed to do a little studying. When I got home, I came in the front door and quickly locked up.

I woke up early to be able to chill a bit before I went to class. I turned on the news. What did I miss overnight? I thought to myself. There were lots of commercials as always, but then, I couldn't believe it. Jaden's photo was on the screen. I frantically searched for the remote to turn the volume up. I finally found it. I cranked it up. He was found dead in an alley outside the bar strip in town called, Pine Street, where all the college kids hand out. He was stabbed with a dagger.

A dagger? I thought… *what an odd weapon! Who carries a dagger?*

They said it wasn't a robbery because nothing was missing, not his cash or watch. That was about all the details they gave. They were asking for any tips from the public that could help. Oh my gosh. NO! I was totally over him, but he died, I would never want that!

I called Mandi and told her. She said she was turning on the news now. Then I called Officer John. I asked him if my stalker could have done this. He was my boyfriend, and we had just broken up. Maybe the stalker didn't know that? Officer John said that could be a real possibility, and they were also looking into that. I was overwhelmed with mixed feelings.

Am I responsible for this? I thought about his poor mom and dad, both were so sweet. I didn't know if I should call them or not. They really liked me, but who knows what Jaden told them about why we broke up.... if he even told them. I decided to call. There were a lot of tears, and I cried, too. Then, they told me they appreciated me calling, and that Jaden thought so much of me, they said. Wow, I didn't know that. I don't think they know we broke up, so I decided not to tell them.

I had to skip Jujitsu that night. There was just too much to take in. I called Levi to let him know. He was really cool about it. But he said he'd miss me. Was he flirting? I had Mandi come over for a girls' night. I didn't want to risk him finding out where she lived if he didn't already, so she came to my place. We watched two of my new favorite movies, "Equalizer," and "Enough," to take my mind off everything. Interesting selection, I guess. It fits the hell I was in right now. It was my turn to pick the movies. Next time it was hers, and I got to say, I love that girl because if I didn't, I would not watch her picks, I thought with a giggle. We had very different tastes in movies.

We chatted about Levi and her boyfriend Steve and dreamed of what the lake would be like. Finally, some things will slow down, but maybe I will finally feel safe!! But poor Jaden would never experience that or anything else again. My mind was all over the place. Watching the movies helped, but then they ended, and I was stuck with this guilt that my stalker could have very well killed him. I didn't know anyone who didn't like Jaden. Maybe another girl he cheated on was responsible? You never know. I hugged Mandi before she left, locked the door after her, and turned on the alarm. I watched her walk to her car from my window to ensure she got in safely. Then I did some studying and went to bed.

Chapter 6: A New Love

The next morning, I planned on going to Jiujitsu before class this time and trying to mix things up. I usually go in the evening. I set my alarm early. When I sat up, I felt hair all over me. Chunks of my hair! I jumped out of bed and felt my head…my hair was cut off, nearly all of it. It was several inches above my shoulders and some shorter pieces than that. Some pieces were cut off above my chin! My hair was nearly reaching my lower back! I ran to a mirror, and I looked horrible. I screamed out loud, and my mom came running downstairs. "Mom, he got in again! He cut all my hair off!" She was in utter shock, just like I was.

I called Officer John, and he came with the forensic team. They dusted everything, then they took my hair and bagged it. They couldn't find any signs of a break-in. How was he getting in? I put on a ballcap and waited for the salon to open. I wanted to be the first one there so they could fix my hair. I got there right at 11 a.m. and told them what happened. My hairdresser, Justine, did an amazing job with my hair. It was very short, but it looked really good. I liked it, not as much as my long hair, but it will grow on me.

I went to school late, and everyone was commenting on my hair. Asking why I cut it off and telling me how cute it was. I just politely smiled at them and finished my day. I had to work right after school, but it was a short shift.

I ended up going to Jiujitsu that evening. When I got there, I saw Levi. He complimented me on my hair, and I told him what happened. He couldn't believe it. This stalker was trying to make me ugly or something. I had the thickest and most beautiful long brown hair. I thought it was my best quality physically. That's probably why he did it.

I went through all the moves with the class as I always started with. Then, the one-on-one practice. With every lesson there, I felt more and more equipped to fight for my life if needed. Without Levi as my mentor, I would be completely lost! Jujitsu makes me feel like I have the power to care for myself should my stalker approach me. Levi walked me to my car after class, just like he did after every class. I'm sure my stalker saw that, too. He worked with me more than anyone else in class. I thought about asking him out, but I didn't have the courage. He most likely had a girlfriend anyway. How could he not? Levi was definitely the whole package.

Then, the unexpected happened. Walking to my car, Levi asked me out!

He doesn't have a girlfriend?

I told him "Yes! I'd love to."

I asked him, "Are you sure, with my stalker and all, do you still want to date me?" "I'm not scared," he replied. "You are totally worth the risk, Mac."

I was so relieved because I liked him. I would say he's cute, but he's more than that, he is beyond hot! Inside and out. He is caring, compassionate, selfless, capable, and enjoyable to look at. I could go on and on. I couldn't tell you how many times I imagined us kissing, especially when he was pinning me down. I couldn't wait to go out with him. He knew I threw knives at home for sport. Like darts but I didn't use darts. He thought we should go to this local place where you can throw axes!

What! I screamed in my head.

I told him I'd love to, and he was excited. I told him I had never been but had heard how fun it was. Then he dropped the bombshell. He said I couldn't be his student anymore if we had a relationship.

A *relationship? Was this happening? Did he really say a relationship?*

But he said he would keep training me, just not at the gym. I was cool with that. Even more cool because I didn't have to pay for lessons anymore either! I would pay him in other ways. The first night, I planned to make him an amazing home-cooked meal. Then I told him I'd teach him to throw knives! We exchanged cell phone numbers, and I got in my car and left.

I drove home, grinning ear to ear. I was so excited. Levi was a real man, the type of man I needed in my life. He was a year older than me and the class before me.

Before I got home, I stopped to get some gas. Something sent chills up my spine. I could feel every hair prickling my back. I used a five-dollar bill to pay for a soda inside, and more chills went up my spine, remembering the five-dollar bill the stalker gave me, the one saying, It was great seeing me, and he'd see me soon or something like that.

What kind of ending was this going to be? I thought to myself. *How will I shake this guy or catch him so he'll be prosecuted and leave me alone?*

I just wanted him out of my life. I was starting to have a bad feeling that this would not end well. There are multiple things that can happen. I let my mind wander, and then I just had to stop. I am safe and having a good time in my life, and that's all I need to worry about. This incredible man just asked me out and was talking about a relationship! Nothing was going to keep this smile from going away!

My mom had the locks changed again, and we have an updated security system now, the one my professor told us to get. I talked my mom into getting a doorknob for the bathroom that needed a key to open so I could shower again without freaking out, and he could never come in while I was showing again. I had a pretty big knife with me everywhere I went and pepper spray (even in the shower). But he's never approached or come close to me except for work and my home. The two places where I spent the most time.

I had a nightmare not too long ago. I was sleeping in bed, and he was standing over me with a pillow in his hands. When I tried to get up, he put the pillow over my face to suffocate me, and I woke up gasping for air.

NO! I decided. No one was going to keep me from doing what I wanted. The fun I wanted to have, the college experience I've always dreamed of, working at a job where I made good money and lived my life. He has no claim on me, and he never will, regardless of how this goes down, I'll be ready.

Turns out I had every reason to freak out. I got home, and both my standing closets were on the floor again, the strap ripped from the wall. And this time, all my clothes were off the hangers and thrown around my room. My once perfectly made bed was a wreck. My pillows were on the floor, the comforter was ripped from the bed onto the floor, and my sheets were torn off halfway. My dresser was nearly empty, and all my clothes were on the floor, too. He obviously just wanted to say, "I was here." That's four times now that this freak has been in my house. With no sign of a break-in. Then it hit me. I learned how to open our garage door without the opener because I was locked out once. I just pulled on the handle at the bottom as hard as I could, and it opened right up! Oh gosh, was he watching me? Is that how he was getting into my home?

I told myself to remember to tell my mom when she got off work. I turned around, and over my headboard, he wrote on my wall, "SEE YOU SOON." I immediately called Officer John. I've been calling him lately per his request. Within about twenty minutes, I heard the sirens, and he was there with a forensics team.

Please, please let them find something to identify this monster, I pleaded in my head.

The forensics team was dusting for prints, taking pictures, and using some kind of blue light on my sheets with the lights off. Looking for semen or something, I guess…. eww. Then again, they would have DNA.

I sent Levi a quick text while they were working and some pictures of my room and texted that I was super freaked out. He wanted to rush over but I told him not too. Officer John took me upstairs to ask me some questions, and then the next thing I knew, Levi was at the front door. He knocked, and I yelled for him to come in. He came straight to me and gave me a big hug. His support meant everything to me. There were a lot of people who just didn't get it, and I was not sure how serious this was.

After a few hours, when the forensics team was finished, and the police left, Levi helped me hang my shirts back on the hangers and hang them up. He re-attached the strap to the wall…not that it did any good last time. Then again, he screwed the straps into a stud, I didn't. He helped me get my clothes back in my dresser, and I noticed my favorite bra was missing. It was my push-up bra with leopard print. I went around to see if anything else was missing.

And there was a few knickknacks that my dad brought me from overseas when he was gone. My remote for the TV vanished, and who knows what else. I was a mess emotionally and couldn't hold it in anymore. I finally broke down and cried in Levi's arms. I'm shocked he still wanted to date me after seeing me "ugly cry." After he left, I locked up and turned on the security system. The cops searched the whole house, including the attic. I felt safe. I wished Levi could have stayed the night, but it just wasn't a good idea.

No one could get ahold of my mom at work. The phones were down or something, and she wasn't answering her cell phone. She probably had it in her purse in her locker. Officer John said he would swing by and tell her what happened so she could come home and be with me.

About 30-minutes later, my mom was home. She embraced me and told me how much she loved me. I cried in her arms, too. I was an emotional train wreck. Luckily, we had paint that matched the basement walls, so my mom and I painted the wording over my headboard. I'm not sure what he used to write it, but it took several coats of paint.

My mom got word on everything going on to my dad's supervisors since she couldn't reach my dad. Once they got word, they gave him orders to return home because of this stalker and how severe his stalking was getting.

My dad got home about a week later. He was excited to show us all the goodies he got for us. He got me my favorite perfume and a few more currencies from Korea. My mom got a beautiful blanket, and my sister got a few trinkets that were really cool. We loved seeing the culture through the souvenirs he brought home and the stories he told. I told him I was taking Jujitsu and dating Levi and that I knew he would love him. My dad's face didn't seem to agree. He didn't like most of my boyfriends and turned out for good reason. But Levi was different. Very different

I told him all about school, especially military science. He really missed us and felt like he missed out on so much. His main concern was with me and the stalker and that it had gone too long, and he would stop it. I wish that was true. I don't think even he could do anything to stop it.

My dad said I needed to stay at home, drop college, and quit my job until things calmed down. "Heck no," I said. I'm going to enjoy my college experience, my friends, Levi, and life in general. Most of what happens is AT HOME, I reminded him. He wasn't happy, but he didn't really have a choice. I wasn't 18 yet, but I was close. I was about six months away.

The next morning, my dad called the landlord about the garage door. He said he'd have someone out to fix it today. Around lunchtime, they showed up, and I showed them how I could open the garage door. They were able to fix the problem and told us we could also lock the garage door on the opening panel.

Genius, I thought.

I had to get ready for work, I made sure all the basement window curtains were completely closed, and I got dressed. I had an eight-hour shift at Sonic. I was opening the store today, so I had to be there by seven am. Heather was opening too. Heather was just the sweetest girl. We became friends quickly when I started working at Sonic. She was the same height as me and had long brown hair like I did until the psycho cut it all off. She had such glowing skin, too. I have to admit I was a bit jealous. She was very pretty. Pretty inside and out.

I hope Harry is in a good mood because I can't deal with his drama today. I shared what happened the night before with Heather, and Harry overheard. I was stunned at what he said. He told me that if I ever saw that son of a bitch here to tell him, and he would go kick his ass waiting while waiting on the police. He said he had no idea what I'd been going through and said if there was anything I needed not to hesitate to ask him. *Oh my gosh, who is this man?* He was super cool the entire shift, and he said he would be walking me to my car at night, and I wasn't to close the restaurant on my own anymore to be safe. Wow, I was so taken back. Especially since the boutique I was working at didn't care at all. I quit working there a few weeks back because of her lack of concern. Lack isn't even the right word. She literally didn't care at all. The owner was a complete Troll!

I got home around three p.m., unlocked the door, turned off the alarm, and then set it again. I hopped in the shower after locking the door and got cleaned up. It always felt so good in the shower after work. The stench of the grease from there was overwhelming. Plus, I had a date tonight with Levi, who had the potential to be the love of my life!

After my shower, I rushed to get ready. I needed the perfect outfit, the most flattering but moveable top so that I could throw axes! I looked all through my closet and couldn't find anything. So, I went to Maurice's really fast and looked at their tops. I found the perfect rusted orange blouse with wiggle room to move around in it. From the mid-chest up, it looked like a corset tying up nearly to the collar bone and it had half sleeves, so not a strappy top or a full-length sleeve, it was in between. I made my purchase and rushed home. I paired it with these flattering green jeans and my Blowfish green shoes. Now hair and makeup. I was still getting used to doing my hair short, but was getting the hang of it. I was finally ready with 30 minutes to spare. It felt like forever waiting for him. I kept checking and re-checking my hair and makeup, then second-guessing my outfit. *Enough!* I look as good as I'm going to, and I need to chill.

Levi picked me up at my house at five o'clock and asked me if I was still up for axe-throwing.

"More than ever," I said, "I have a target in mind, so I can't miss," I giggled.

Levi laughed, "Yes, you sure do." he grinned.

We drove to the city to the axe-throwing establishment. We had so much fun. And I got a bullseye on my first throw. Wow! I couldn't believe it, but I played it cool. Then I got another one! Levi said, "have you done this before?" laughing. My ego was getting big. He was really good too. I'm a competitive person. That turns some guys off, but not Levi, he was competitive, too. But neither of us were competitive in a crazy way. I took in every moment and detail as he made his throws. He was hitting bullseyes, too. He was a masterpiece.

We had a few more drinks and headed out. I used my fake ID, of course, and Levi actually had one too. We laughed so much. I couldn't believe how much we had in common. Likes, dislikes, parents, music, being the younger sibling, and so much more.

He drove me home and walked me to the door. To my surprise, he laid a soft and sweet kiss on my lips. I parted my mouth just a little, inviting him in for a deeper kiss, and we made out for a minute.

"I've wanted to kiss you since I started taking classes with you, Levi," I said. "This is like my fantasy come true. I wanted to know what it would be like to kiss you, especially when you had me pinned down." I gushed.

He said, "I thought the same thing, and it was so hard to stay professional."

I smiled really big and giggled.

Mac...you did NOT just giggle like a schoolgirl. I reprimanded myself.

Levi thought it was cute. I was so embarrassed.

I invited him inside and we talked and kissed some more; it was amazing! I was really into him. After about an hour, we made plans for our next date at a drive-in movie theater next week. But he said he wanted to come over in a couple of days and work with me on Jujitsu to keep my skills sharp. I was so very happy to do so. I told him on Wednesday, I had a class that the professor had to cancel, so I'd be free after 11 a.m. I had to work at four p.m., though. So, we made plans for 11 a.m. I couldn't wait.

I woke up early and immediately smiled, reminiscing about last night with Levi. I couldn't wait for Mandi to wake up so I could tell her everything that happened! I sent her a text to call me when she wakes up.

When she woke up, she called me and I told her all about our date, our kiss, or multiple kisses. She was so happy for me, and still pissed about how both Tommy and Jaden treated me. She said she's so happy I'm finally with a keeper, and then she said, "He's not too hard to look at either." She laughed. I told her I don't even think of Tommy anymore, and Jaden, I wanted to dump him anyway. But sadly, Jaden is dead. I still felt horrible. I may not have wanted to be his girlfriend anymore, but his death was still a tragedy. There was still no news or updates to go on to find his killer.

I just couldn't stop talking about Levi. She said she was so happy for me. She said I deserve a good man, and one willing to date me with a psycho in the mist whose last boyfriend was possibly killed by him. I told her I totally agreed. He was like my hero. I told her I was so happy that she and Steve were still doing well and that Levi and I were dating, at that fun, beginning. dating phase. Finally, both of us had amazing relationships with good guys. We planned on having a double date so we could all meet.

I started getting ready for class. I had a full load, which meant five classes. It was an all-day affair, I guess it's supposed to be. I did get one long break because of the way I had to set up my schedule. I usually used that time to study or complete assignments. Then, at night, I worked. I had to continue to study and do assignments. Finding time to be with Levi was difficult, but I had it at the top of my list. And Mandi of course, but she totally understood because she had the same busyness.

I loved Military Science. It was my favorite class. We even went into the gun range, where we were all issued rifles and briefly instructed on how to use them. The girls got sandbags to help hold and steady the rifle. The guys didn't get one. So, I didn't want a sandbag. I didn't want to kick butt shooting, and then the guys say it was because I was using the sandbag. I was too competitive. This was the first time that I ever shot a gun. My first shot was right in the center of the target's head! Then multiple to the chest as instructed. I earned expert marksmanship!

I went to Levi's house because I had a little time in my day. We talked and made out and, of course, worked on Jujitsu. I think I'm in love with this man. How is it that I'm falling in love so fast? We've had one date. But I guess we have a history since before we started dating.

My heart melts just looking at him. Jiujitsu is really fun now. When he pinned me down, I didn't try to get him off me; instead, I looked deep into his gorgeous brown eyes, telling him to kiss me with my eyes, and he did, and we kissed softly, and Levi took one of his hands, holding up his body up with the other, and brushed my hair out of my face and held my head. The kiss was amazing. He's such a good kisser. After the nice, long kiss, Levi told me to get serious. I needed to learn all I could. I didn't want to, I just wanted to keep kissing him. But yes, I needed to get serious. And I did. I could get away from him with each stance he took to attack me. And he wasn't making it easy on me either. I learned how to choke out the driver in a car if I was in the back seat with the driver's seat belt. How to get out of restraints. Also, how to buck someone off if they are on top of me. How to put an assailant into a choke hold until they passed out. How to break fingers. How to get out of a chokehold. And several other tactics. Basically, I learned a ton. But I had to keep practicing regularly until it was muscle memory.

After hanging out with Levi, and doing Jiujitsu, I had to speed back to campus. I totally lost track of time. But I made it to my next class in time.

Whew, I thought. *That was too close.* I need to stay on campus during my break.

About a week later, I invited Levi to come on campus for Military Science to watch me repel from a five story building. He said he'd love to come, and he did. I repelled multiple times. They even played the theme song from "Mission Impossible" as we repelled. It was such an adrenaline rush, and I loved it. I loved heights, and repelling was like a drug! I ran back up the stairs and repelled again and again. There was a huge crowd watching us. I went upside down a few times and crawled down the side of the building like spiderman. It was one of the best experiences of my life! Mandi and my mom and dad came to watch too. I was so happy to have my dad physically at one of my events! Levi and I locked eyes a few times. He was watching with glee at how much fun I was having for once. And I was! I was having the time of my life and never once thought about my stalker! When it was over, Levi noticed I was bleeding. The building was stone and brick, so I scratched up my hands and one of my elbows, and a knee. I told him it was nothing and so worth it. I wish I could do this every day!

It was Wednesday, and it was more Jiujitsu time. I went to Levi's, and we worked on Jiujitsu and made out for a little bit.

Then, right in the middle of a move, he asked me if we could make it official that we were boyfriend and girlfriend and wouldn't date other people. I lost my hold on his arm and just stared deep into his eyes. "Is that a no?" He hesitantly asked.

I kissed him big, and said, "I've been waiting for you to ask me to be your girlfriend the moment I laid eyes on you."

We embraced and kissed each other some more. Then I smacked his butt and ran. He chased me down and smacked my butt back. Then he picked me up, and then fireman carried me into the living room and plopped me down on his couch. I sat up, and he got on his knees, and we kissed again. I told Levi I better get home. I had a ton of homework and studying to do. We kissed goodbye, and I left, still having butterflies in my stomach.

I'm actually Levi's girlfriend now! I still couldn't believe it.

I was driving my sister's car because my car was in the shop. I dropped her off at work, then headed home to study. It was dark, the moon was covered with clouds. It was hard to see.

As I was driving, this car started flashing its lights at me, and I couldn't see what the car was behind me, was it him? It had to be. I turned down some random road, and it was a dead end. My heart was pounding out of my chest. The car stayed behind me with the lights on, and I couldn't see it. Nobody got out of the car, and we both just sat there, and I wondered, is this it? Is this where he's going to abduct me or kill me? *Hell no,* I thought.

I grabbed my knife and pepper spray; I felt better with my weapons. I started to feel a little better, but still waited. The car finally turned around and left. It was pitch black, but I could see a little bit of the color, it was a bright blue color. It wasn't the same as my stalker's car. Did he get a new car? Who was that?

I immediately drove to where my sister was working, she worked at a pizza joint. When I arrived, I saw the car there. I ran inside with my knife open and out and in my hand, and I saw Michelle talking to her boyfriend, Ron. I told her what had happened and that the car was in the parking lot of her work. Then Ron chimed in and apologized and said it was him. He thought it was my sister because I was driving her car. Thank God, I said to myself.

He apologized, "I know you have a stalker, Mac. That had to be really scary. I thought about approaching you but thought that might scare you and you might pepper spray me or something, so I just drove off to tell Michelle what happened."

"It's OK," I said. "And yes, had you approached me like that in the dark, you would have been pepper sprayed," I said, laughing.

I told Michelle I was headed home to study, and I'd pick her up in a few hours and thanked her for letting me borrow her car.

I was really scared, and now I know not to turn down random roads! I called Levi and told him what happened. He was relieved it wasn't my stalker, but he pointed out that going off the main road was a huge mistake, always stay on the road or pull into a parking lot or police station…never down a random road. And I know these things too, but I couldn't think at that moment. I hope that next time, I will be able to be smart and not stupid while driving down some off-road.

Levi suggested following me around town at a distance and waiting for the stalker's car to show up. Then he would follow him and get his address and plate number to the police. That was genius! Assuming the stalker didn't know what kind of car he drove. Levi is so sweet. And that was a good plan. But I didn't want him to get hurt. He said he was going to do it anyway.

So, Levi and I left simultaneously, I headed to the library. He stayed several cars behind me, sure enough, the description of my stalker's car pulled out and got two cars behind me. Right in front of Levi. The blueish-gray car with a dent in the fender. Levi saw it, too, I had him on the speaker in my car. I told him not to approach him. I begged him. I didn't want him to end up like Jaden. Then Levi said that the car didn't have a license plate. *WHAT*? I thought. No way!!! How has he not been pulled over yet? And how are we supposed to figure out who he was? He couldn't get a good look at his face. He was wearing a ball cap but was close enough to snap a few pictures with his phone. I begged Levi to stop and turn off somewhere before the stalker realized what he was doing…and he did. My heart was pounding. I asked Levi to send me the photos so

I could send them to Officer John. And then started thinking, why weren't the police doing this? Why put Levi in danger?

Chapter 7: Summertime at the Lake

I did it! I earned straight As in college, and now it is time to graduate!

Graduation was boring, for sure. Mandi and I tried to stay together so we could walk together, but we were seated according to our last names. Mine was J, and she was L...So close! We did have beach balls we were bouncing around, but guess who kept catching them and popping them? My Chemistry teacher. Go figure. We also handed a roll of pennies to the principals when we got our diplomas. When we shook hands, we would slide the roll into their hands. Everyone did it, and the principal just put them in his pockets. I hoped they were wearing belts! Ha ha ha. They had to keep taking turns because of all the penny rolls. It was hilarious!

Levi came to my graduation. When they finished the I letter, J was next. So I stood up and got in line. One by one, we walked closer to the stage. Finally, it was my turn. I stepped up the stairs and walked to the center stage. I shook hands and slipped the roll of pennies to my principal, trying desperately not to laugh. Then we posed for a picture with my diploma, and I walked off stage, moving my tassel to the opposite side, then I went back to my seat. HURRY, I kept thinking. Then, I waited for Mandi to walk. I stood up and hooted and hollered! She looked at me and smiled. We weren't allowed to do that, but I didn't care. I am done with this school now.

When it was over, I hugged Mandi, and we took a selfie. Then Levi found us, and my parents took pictures of all of us. It was finally over!

I was really looking forward to the Lake, we were only a couple weeks out. I told Levi that I was going to the lake for the summer with my friends to work at a place called Shooters 21! This was my first time moving out, and I was still 17, which was several months before I turned 18. To my surprise, he said, "I don't want to invite myself, but may I come with you? I can get my own place and work with you at Shooters 21. I'd feel so much better about your safety if I were there too."

"Heck yes," I said, "I would love that!" I said, "I was actually just about to ask you if you wanted to come, but I wasn't sure you could because of your job." He told me he is a good friend with the owner of the jiujitsu gym. A summer away, he said, would be no big deal. *Ahhhh,* I was so excited! Of course, I had to clear it with my roommates, but I knew they wouldn't mind. I'd rather him stay with us than get his own place. He said he would definitely be open to staying with us! And my roommates liked Levi. Besides, he could offer them some free Jujitsu lessons.

The weeks flew by, and it was time to head to the lake! I was so excited! My parents were not. They were concerned about my safety, and my dad was not happy about the living arrangements, even though Levi had a separate room. But I also knew I'd be safer with Levi staying with us. He was slowly learning to let go. I know how hard that is for him. He's a control freak. But he couldn't do much, seeing I was 17. Legally, in my state, you can move out at 17. My mom was more chilled about it.

I was a graduate, had some college under my belt, and I would have the best summer ever with my best friends Mandi, Misty, and Kaye! And now Levi! Levi, Steve, and a couple of their friends went house to house with the U-Haul, helping us pack up everything. We had a futon, a couch, beds, dishes, and all the other things we needed. They came to the lake and moved everything in for us, after we cleaned up.

We were renting a three-bedroom trailer that Misty's dad owned. It was right next door to him. Apparently, the person living there before was in jail and forgot to tell people about his dog. So, we had a lot of cleaning to do. There was petrified dog poop all over the carpets. I went into my closet, and there was a hole where squirrels were getting in, and there were a man's "whities" shoved in the hole. After we cleaned the carpets, we had to clean out all the drawers, and Kaye almost got stabbed by a needle. It was a syringe. Probably used to shoot up. Basically, it was a dump, but it was a place to sleep while we worked our butts off at Shooters 21! Kaye and Misty shared a room, Mandi and I shared a room, and

Levi had his own room. And when Steve visited, I'd sleep with Levi, so Mandi and Steve could have privacy.

Shooters 21 was huge and always packed! It was on the lake and had a nightclub, gas pump, fine dining, an off-the-menu outdoor lower deck restaurant, a Tiki bar for nighttime, sand volleyball, and a gift shop. My roommates, Misty, Mandi, and Kaye were waitresses in the daytime on the lower deck restaurant and fine dining in the evenings. I was docking, tying up boats, and pumping gas. I made pretty good tips. I fell in the water a few times while docking boats. That's scary. You can easily get smashed, so you swim as far down as you can under the boat and come up on the other side. But the water was a nice cool off in the heat! Levi was a waiter at the lower deck restaurant, and he also was a bouncer at the nightclub three to four nights a week, even though he was 19, they were desperate, and Levi had the muscle and skill to be a great bouncer.

My manager, Rick, and I were talking and hanging out. He liked pulling girls aside to 'talk' when he just wanted to flirt. I didn't mind it gave me a break from the sun. After we talked for a few minutes, he pulled out this binder. In it were all the confiscated IDs from the nightclub. He gave me one that looked like me, besides the fact it said she was 5'4 and I was 5'10. He gave us all one so we could go to the bars and dance clubs. He said we could use it anywhere but there. I already had a fake ID, but two is always good in case one gets confiscated.

Misty was 20, the oldest. She turned 21 after two weeks of getting to the lake. So, we of course, had a huge celebration for her! We now had access to tons of alcohol. Our fridge was full of it. There wasn't much food.

We had a lot of parties at our place. Even some of the guys we knew from college drove down, and my roommates' boyfriends came on the weekends when they weren't working, sometimes bringing friends. They kept themselves busy until we were done with our shifts. It was about a three-hour drive, and they stayed with us and partied. It got packed. People were sleeping on couches, on the floor, and where they could lay down.

One night, instead of partying at our place, we went to this club called The Poop Deck, clever name, and they were known for their amazing dance music and drinks. I went there the most. We would also eat on the deck some nights. We often went to the same club, but sometimes we split up too. I could never get Mandi to dance.

She hated it, even drinking. So sometimes she went with another group to a different bar. Levi, of course, went to the same clubs I did. He is an amazing dancer. We had a blast there. Burned a ton of calories dancing, too. We had so much fun! My fake ID worked like a charm. I also don't think anyone cared.

Money was tight at first, but luckily all the rent and utilities were split 4 ways. I had to learn how to live on my own for the first time, and it was a little difficult. I drove to Burger King just to get the $1 chicken sandwich and water for dinner. At work, we would eat the meals that were taken back to the kitchen because they messed up an order, instead of throwing the food away, the dock crew, including myself, ate it. But after a few weeks of working, money wasn't as tight.

The best part was that there was no stalker, or so I thought. After about three weeks of living at the lake, I left work, and there was a note on my windshield. I removed it from under my window wiper and opened it up. It had little squares with letters on them, and it looked like it had been cut out of a magazine and glued to the paper. *How cliche*, I thought. I read the note, and it said, "You can't hide from me." I just stared at the piece of paper and read it repeatedly. I felt a hand on my shoulder, and my heart flip-flopped, I was startled and jumped. It was just a co-worker named Jami, and she wanted to make sure I was OK. She said I looked like I saw a ghost. I told her I was OK and crumpled up the letter. She said "OK" and left unsurely.

I guess John Doe, the stalker, thought that my going to the lake was hiding from him, and it kind of was. What do I do now? I went to the police station, and was hoping they could get fingerprints off the crumpled letter, oh why did I crumple it? What if I ruined the evidence?

When I got to the police station, I talked to Officer Cole, and I explained the situation, including where I lived and went to school and everything the stalker had done. I asked him if he could connect with Officer John in Warrensburg. Then I showed him the letter. They needed my fingerprints to rule mine out from what they might find. After a long wait, they came out to tell me that it looked as though he wore gloves, there was not a single fingerprint, except mine. But they kept the letter for evidence. I asked if I could take a picture of it, and they said that was fine. They also let the police department back home know about the letter. I was very appreciative.

So now the creep is here. Did he move down here? Could he even be employed by Shooters 21 like me? Did he just drive down to drop off the note? Will he be at my work? Will I be serving him as a waitress or docking his boat? I have no idea who this guy is. All I know is that he knew where I was, and he was still at it. Thankfully, we had a lot of male presence around our trailer.

My guy friends and my roommate's boyfriends were there a lot. Levi was a constant presence, too. Nevertheless, it was quite scary to have that note on my windshield. And how cliche with the cut letters out of a magazine. I showed Mandi, Misty, Kaye, and Levi the picture I took of the letter before the police put it in evidence. They knew I had a stalker, but we all assumed that it would be over once we moved to the lake.

They said this was bullshit, and we would find out who it was and put an end to it. They always have my back. So do the guys. I had acted strong for so long I was exhausted. I finally felt like I could just let go of the tough act and break down because I really needed to. I do feel safe because I had three roommates, plus Levi and anybody else hanging out there. I was mainly at work all day. It was nothing to work a 12-hour shift. It was actually pretty standard. I guess I could still get abducted at work, especially on the dock. Sometimes I had to tie up a boat solo because we were busy and short-staffed. He could easily pull me in his boat and take off. I had to quit thinking of all the "what ifs" in my brain.

I still loved the lake and the fun I was having. And I know my roommates meant well, but I seriously doubt we would be able to figure out who he was. I thought and thought so hard about who it could be. Maybe a guy friend I have, maybe a stranger who just saw me somewhere and was intrigued. Maybe at the bar back home or someone I served at Sonic. Maybe even someone from one of my high school classes. It seriously could be anybody. All I knew was that it was a man based on the silhouette I saw that one night outside my home and the quick glimpse I got of him when he was following me. He had short hair. That was all I had to go on.

With Levi, I felt safe. Safer than I have in a long time. I laid down with Levi that night and just let him hold me. I felt so safe in his arms. He had a pistol he brought with him. I jokingly asked him if jujitsu wasn't enough. He laughed. He said he preferred not to get that close to him, then again, he wouldn't mind beating the crap out of him. He was worried he may have a gun. And he very well might.

I absolutely refused to let this stalker ruin my summer! I felt safe, and he could leave all the notes on my car's windshield that he wanted to. I was rarely home alone. Someone was always there, and at work, there were lots of people around. I decided I was going just to ignore it. Or at least try to ignore it. I put on a brave face but was seriously scared of this guy. Who wouldn't be?

After working the docks, parking and gassing up boats, I was asked to temporarily work in the gift shop. Some girl quit at the last minute. It was a nice break from the heat, for sure! It was really boring, though…and no tips! After that, I did both, depending on the day. Then, they needed help with fine dining and the cigar stand. So, I did that too. It was so fancy there. I'd cut cigars for customers. I was also the hostess and showed customers to their tables. We were always packed in there. It pretty much required a reservation. I loved it! I was pretty much a floater at this point. I did just about everything except work the night club or bartending because of my age. I got to work with my roommates more too, and of course, Levi.

One time, when I was hosting, a table of people thought I was a waitress, and their plates needed to be moved off their table, so they just started putting them on another table, a table that I needed for waiting customers. So, I went there to grab their plates to help the bus team, and they chewed me out. They told me that I was too lazy to get their plates when they finished. They said they were watching me and waiting, but I was just walking around, not doing anything. I told them I wasn't a waitress and was just helping the bussing team. The guy who was harassing me just rolled his eyes.

I went back to the kitchen and started tearing up. Which is so not like me, but with everything going on, being tough 24/7 was becoming impossible. It was such a long day, and that did me in. Misty and Mandi were waitressing and saw me in the kitchen with tears in my eyes. I told them what happened, and they said they would take care of it. Misty went out there and talked to the people at the table and told them that their behavior was unacceptable and they'd have to leave if it kept up. They later apologized to me and said they didn't know I was the hostess. I told them that, regardless, what they said was not okay. They shouldn't treat anyone that way. I apologized that we were short-staffed, and it was extremely busy, but we were all doing the best we could. Then I just turned around and walked off.

I just took a couple to their table, and on my way back to the hostess spot, I had a guy stop me. He asked if I could just get his wife some water from the bar, which was beyond packed. I told him sure, just a moment. The bartender was a friend, so he hooked me up and served me before others waiting. When I gave his wife her water, he tipped me $10! I even got tips at the cigar booth, sometimes a few bucks, average five dollars, and once $50!

Are you kidding me? $50! I thought

I would cut the cigars that they bought, they even had Cuban cigars, which I told my manager I wouldn't sell, a Criminal Justice major and all. He said that was fine. If someone wanted a Cuban just to come get him, he'd sell it. I had this really cool lighter, too, to light their cigars. I got tipped for that, too. Seriously, best job ever! I had so much fun with new friends too.

We had "locals-only parties" that were just for people who lived at the lake and worked the bars in town. We had some awesome pool parties!

When I finished my shift in fine dining, I went to the Tiki bar, waiting for Levi to get off work. My uniform was a white top and black skirt or pants. Today, I wore a white spaghetti strap tank top under my blouse, and a long black skirt. I took off my blouse because it was so hot. The tiki bar was a little hut, and the drinks were served there. There was music for dancing and sometimes live music.

That night, a bachelor was out with his buds, and at the tiki bar, the MC thought it would be fun to have him sit in the middle of the dance floor and have women come and dance for him. Most were grinding on him and stuff like that.

Tacky, I thought.

When they finished, I thought it would be fun, so I got on the dance floor, and the MC announced me by name, saying, "And here we have our very own Mac. She's a member of our Shooters 21 family! Give it up for her!" He said. There was applause and hooting and hollering.

He keyed the music, and I started dancing. Not grinding on him like the other girls, but just dancing really close to his chair, a tad seductively. Not stripper like, but close. I loved dancing, and I liked seducing men for some reason. After the song ended, I congratulated him. He asked me to stay and dance again, but I was tired. One of his buds offered me $20, and one of his other buds added another $20.

I wouldn't pass that up, so I told the MC to put on another song. "Are you guys ready for some sugar?" He asked. Then he played "Pour Some Sugar on Me by Def Leppard!

Yes!

I loved that song. So, I danced close to his chair again. I was really getting into it. It was an awesome song, and I loved dancing to it. When it was over, I took the $40 and said, "Congratulations again." They asked me to come back and do one more song. I said that I needed to meet up with my boyfriend. They said, "What, you have a boyfriend, man!" I laughed, and I went into the ladies' room and used the bathroom.

I was washing my hands when a girl told me that I could really dance. I said, "thank you, that is really sweet of you to say." And I walked out of the bathroom and checked my phone, wondering if Levi was off yet, and went back to the Tiki bar. He was there.

Finally, I thought.

I went and sat by him, and he said, "You have some major moves, Mac, which I already knew, but watching you is a whole other story.

"Oh my gosh," I squealed, putting both hands over my eyes. "You saw me dancing for that bachelor?"

"Yes," he said. "And I have to admit I am a little jealous."

I said he had nothing to be jealous of. I told him I'd give him a closer dance whenever we got home. He smiled really big.

"I can't wait," he said.

"So, let's get on the dance floor."

Levi and I danced a few songs together, our bodies touching. I was trying to seduce him, and it worked. He turned me around and danced behind me, pulling my body into his to one of the songs with a slower, swaying-like beat. I had major butterflies. He started kissing the back of my neck, I turned around and kissed him, and we decided to take it somewhere else.

Levi and I sat on the edge of the boat dock with our feet in the water, sharing our days and how fun the summer has been. He was off from the nightclub tonight, so we had an evening to just chill. I told him about hopping around all day, and I was wiped. He laughed and said, "Aren't you used to being busy, Mac?"

I laughed and said, "Yes, I am, but this peaceful night was just what I needed."

He joked more about the tiki bar where I was dancing for the Bachelor, and said I put some major moves on that guy.

"You were seductive, Mac."

I laughed, and then I pushed him into the water. His head popped out of the lake, and he said, laughing, "What was that for?"

"It sounded like you needed to cool off a bit," I said, laughing so hard I almost peed my pants. He climbed back up on the dock, shaking the hair out of his face, and said, "now it's your turn."

I got up and tried to run, but he caught me, his arms were around my waist, and I squealed as he threw us both in the lake. We were both laughing so hard. He helped me climb back up on the dock in my long, wet skirt, and then pulled himself up. The lake water felt good.

We went back to our trailer and dried off. I noticed I actually got a tan as I was peeling my wet clothes off to dry off. I usually don't tan; I have such pale skin. I burn, then white again.

I turned on some music and started singing in the living room, waiting for Levi to dry off and get dressed. Suddenly, he pressed his body up behind me. Then he started moving his hands down low, a little too low, but I let it go. He was seriously turning me on. I was getting butterflies again. The song was over, and I turned around to kiss him. I was horrified. I screamed!

Chapter 8: Stalker Strikes Again

I was dancing with some strange man. He was probably in his late 20s, and he was wearing a polo shirt and jeans. He had a long face with stubble or a five o'clock shadow, it was hard to tell. But it wasn't Levi!

I screamed at the top of my lungs, "Levi!"

He put his hand around my mouth and started dragging me towards the door, but when he heard Levi in the other room, he ran out the door. That had to have been my stalker!

Levi ran out of his room half-dressed. "Mac, what's wrong?" he asked. I started crying and fell to my knees. Levi squatted down. I told him that I was dancing, like we were at the Tiki bar. I think he was there watching. He came into the room, pressed his body behind me, and was dancing with me. The way we were. He was lowering his hands on me, which I thought was weird.

"I thought it was you!" I cried. "So, I let him."

I cried even more. I danced for the remainder of the song with him. Then I said that I turned around to kiss who I thought was you, but it was some strange man. When I screamed, he put his hand over my mouth and started dragging me to the door. Then I think he heard you, and he ran out the door.

"Mac, I am so sorry," he said.

He ran to the door to see if he could see anything.

"He's long gone, Mac. You're safe now," he assured me.

Levi called the police. Office Cole arrived shortly after. They came out with a sketch artist. I described him the best I could. It happened so fast but describing him was hard. I'll never forget his face. The sketch artist showed me the portrait, which looked like him, but it wasn't perfect. We had been over the sketch four times already, and I was tired.

It was his eyes, they were crazed. I couldn't get that to show in the sketch. I couldn't explain it and just wanted them to leave, so I told them it was good. I asked if I could take a picture of it so I could show it to my roommates, and they let me. They said they were going to send it to the Warrensburg police station and also the news down here at the lake as a person of interest. The police asked if he did anything else. I said no, he just danced with me from behind and was moving his hands pretty low. Then, after I screamed, he put his hand around my mouth and tried to drag me out of the trailer. He was really brave to do that. Levi could have come out any second.

He was getting really risky!

Michelle came down on Friday and was leaving on Saturday afternoon. I had asked for Friday off, and shockingly, they gave it to me. Michelle is the opposite of me. I have dark hair, and she has blonde hair. She loves being active, and we actually get along now, which is nice. Michelle and I decided to rent a jet ski. We were going to ride around, stop at a restaurant for lunch, and then return the jet ski. We rented it for two hours. It was so much fun until she did something that sent us both flying off the jet ski. I hit the water so hard I got knocked out. When I came to, my sister was screaming because a boat was headed my way. I have no idea how we were so far away from each other. I started waving my arms, and they saw me and went around me. We both swam to the jet ski. We decided to turned it in early, and I drove it this time. We both were hurting pretty badly. Hitting the water like that was like hitting concrete. My head was killing me. After we turned in the jet ski, we had lunch...Not at Shooters 21. I wanted to go to a different lakeside restaurant. It was a nice, peaceful day.

I told her about the note on my car, and the dancing, and she just couldn't believe it. She asked me if I had called the cops, and I told her that I had gone there and given it to them. Unfortunately, there were no fingerprints. They did keep it as evidence, though. And they came to the trailer after the dancing incident, and had me work with a sketch artist. I asked if she wanted to see the sketch, and she said, yes. I showed it to her and she was glad everyone knew what he looked like now! She told me to be careful and not go anywhere alone, including where I lived. I told her that on the rare occasion, no roommates or friends were there, I usually just hang out at Shooters where I work. She said good, and she was worried about me.

I told her that I was worried, too. I was scared but I refused to let him rule my life. She told me my pride might get me hurt or worse, or even killed. She had a point. I almost just want this guy to come for me as the last hit just to get it over with. I felt like my chances of coming out on top were pretty good, given my training. Then again, he was a man and bigger than me. He is so stealthy when breaking in, giving me notes, and coming to my work.

I really just wanted to have a great summer and not stress about whether today is the day he attacks me. We had a decent-sized party that night. I'm talking about pulling people out of gutters and getting them back to our trailer, all of it. We had a wooden rotting deck. I wasn't sure how many people that it would hold, but there were many people out there. My sister puked all over my carpet. I was ticked but had to laugh. She's a lightweight. The next morning Michelle looked like crap, and I'm sure she felt that way too. "Good morning, sunshine," I said sarcastically. She shot me a dirty look and went to the bathroom to get a shower.

It seemed like our shower was constantly being used. It was really difficult when we all worked the same shifts. We all had to come home and shower before going to fine dining. And it wasn't just the shower. Our window air units were constantly running. And we were still sweating. So, us girls started doing our make up in the parking lot before our shifts, where it was cool, and they started just wearing ponytails because their hair was still wet. I don't have that problem now. My hair was so short, but it was growing out, and it dried faster.

I had a dock shift that morning, so I was getting ready for work in my room. Michelle got out of the shower and got dressed in my room. She made a quick five-minute face and I gave her a hug goodbye. I had to get to work because the gas pumps open earlier than Shooters. I was the first to leave. "Love you", she yelled on her way out the door.

"Love you too," I yelled back. "Be careful driving home," I said.

Levi was returning from checking the mail so I gave him a big kiss and told him I'd see him later. Steve was there now, he came early Saturday morning. He was too tired to drive after work Friday night. Which worked out because Michelle was there. They were staying another day, so Steve and some friends were at the house all day. I was using Levi's room while Steve was there.

We all worked until dinner time, then had to come home and shower and change clothes. When we walked into the trailer, there was something red all over the carpet. Steve spilt a bottle of Red Tattoo on the kitchen carpet while we were all at work. He thought it would be funny to tape out a human body and make it like a crime scene. We were all pissed at first. But then we found it pretty funny and creative. However, it kind of freaked me out. I just had a flash of me dead there on the floor. *Ugh*. I must stop letting this guy get to me. He'll screw up, I just know it, then the police can get him. Steve must have seen me space out because he immediately apologized to me and started pulling the tape off the carpet. He said, "Mac, I'm so sorry, I didn't mean to freak you out. I know what you've been going through. I'll get this cleaned up." I told him I was OK and it was funny, but I couldn't help but see my body there on the floor." He apologized again and I told him it was totally OK. It was funny.

Levi and I both had the night off, so we wanted to take advantage of the privacy at the trailer. I put on some music. I loved dancing with Levi, this jerk stalker wouldn't take that from me. We sat around and listened to a few upbeat songs, we sang and danced a little along to some of them. Then, a few slow songs came on, so we got up to dance. "Amazed" came on by Lonestar. I'm not a country music fan, but I love this song. The lyrics and the way it's sung make you feel what true love is.

We slowly danced and he whispered, "this should be our song." I agreed.

Then, "In Your Eyes" by Peter Gabriel came on, and I whispered to Levi, "This should be our song, too." He agreed. The lyrics of "In Your Eyes" were also so beautiful and perfectly written, especially for this moment we were sharing. I started quietly humming the song under my breath, and Levi told me, "You have a beautiful voice, Mac." I laughed and said, "I was humming."

My face was red with embarrassment. I didn't realize he could hear me that well. "I didn't know you could sing and dance like you do." He said. "Well, I'm full of surprises!" I said back.

I was moving my body and my hips, totally trying to seduce him, and it was working! He slowly started to raise my skirt as we danced, feeling my hips move. How can one small thing turn me on so badly?

I told him, "You are totally turning me on right now, feeling me up like that."

"I am?" he said with a grin.

"Good, it's working' then." He said.

After dancing, we went to my room, and he laid me down on my bed, he slowly got on top of me, and we kissed. One of those, I want you now kisses. Then he got behind me, and I turned to face him. We were just holding each other. He told me he loved me, and I told him I loved him too. He brushed the hair out of my face, which was always in my face. I was trying to get used to this new short hair. Then we made out for a bit.

"Have I ever told you that you are an amazing kisser?" I asked Levi. "No." he said. "Maybe you should tell me again." He grinned. "You are an amazing kisser," I whispered. He whispered back, "You are an amazing kisser as well."

We made out some more, our kissing getting harder and harder. I ran my hand through his hair and down his back. He held my neck and gently started kissing it. I was getting so turned on again, and I could tell he was too.

We decided it was time for bed. We were both exhausted, but we had an amazing evening together. We didn't get the opportunity too often with our work shifts. I thought about asking him to make love to me, but I couldn't. I just wasn't ready. I wanted to wait until I was married, but I didn't know if I could do that with Levi. I wanted him so badly. Then I thought, how special would that be? For your first time to be with your husband. Levi was about to open my bedroom door and go to his room to sleep himself, and I said, "wait."

"What's up, Mac?" he replied.

"Stay with me tonight. Just hold me. I don't want tonight to end."

He turned around and came back into my room. I told him, "lets go to your room so Mandi doesn't have to see us in bed together. He agreed, and we went to his room. I jumped in his bed. He removed his jeans and shirt, but kept his boxers on, then he crawled into my bed. He looked so hot in his boxers. We kissed and then fell asleep in each other's arms.

The next day, I was on cloud nine, despite the twelve-hour workday ahead of me. Levi and I woke up and started getting ready for work. He told me that last night was one of the best nights he'd ever had. I told him I felt the same. He was picking up a shift waiting at the Lower Dock restaurant, then he had to be the bouncer at the nightclub after that. I was docking boats, then I needed to drive home and takie a shower, then get all dolled up as usual for hosting in fine dining.

Misty and Kaye were having to do the same. We would drive back and go upstairs to fine dining, which stayed open until one a.m. That meant that Levi and I should be getting off at the same time. I was finally at work and was docking boats. I saw Mandi waitressing at the Lower Dock restaurant, and I gave her a wave. We would work together that night in fine dining in a couple hours, after the Lower Dock closed. She was stuck closing. At least she'd have the shower and trailer to herself.

I would be hosting again, and run the cigar stand. We were all getting wiped out. But they promised after Thursday, the load would lighten. Several staff members had to enroll in classes, then come back. They lived further away than we did. As the summer dwindled away, people continued quitting, leaving us with few employees. So, that left us working more than twelve hours some days now.

I should ask for a raise, I thought.

Levi started waiting tables again because we didn't have enough waiters while still being a bouncer at night. It was no longer fun.

We were all exhausted, and it was so hot. I loved the glow of my skin for once, though. I tanned even more over the last few weeks. For some reason, it made me feel more attractive than my porcelain skin.

I was docking boats, then, I saw Levi walking down the docks and thought he was coming to say hi. He said he was sent here to help dock the boats, and I was supposed to train him.

"Oh," I said. "It looks like I will get to teach you something now," I laughed.

I showed him the ropes and how to tie the boats down with bumpers. I made sure he knew what to do if he ever fell in. He picked it up after two boats. He's my rockstar. We worked together the whole day, and it was so much fun. Then he went to the nightclub, and I went home. They ended up having another girl hosting fine dining tonight, which was awesome, I needed some sleep.

I got to the trailer, and shockingly, it was just me. No roommates, no guests. Just me. I was a little freaked out, but I had my pepper spray. I decided to call it a night. I texted Levi goodnight and turned off my light. I had my favorite pajamas on. It was basically a dress but super strappy and oh-so-soft. It was so dark in my room, and the trailer. I couldn't see anything. Good for sleeping, I thought to myself. Hopefully, no one will bring a party over here tonight. I fell asleep quickly. Something woke me up a few hours later. I could feel the shoulder strap of my pajamas being pulled down, and soft kisses on my shoulder. "Levi, back so soon?" I asked.

But he didn't say anything. Then he slowly lowered my other strap and kissed that shoulder. "Levi?"

I grabbed my phone and turned on the flashlight, and it was that weird man again! My stalker!

I screamed and grabbed the pepper spray, and I sprayed him right in the face, also getting some in my face. It burned my eyes and made me cough. He started coughing, too, trying to manage his way out of my room. I screamed as loud as I could. I called 911 and texted Levi "911…he came back" while I was on the line with the police. I told them it was a break-in, and I was assaulted. The next thing I knew I heard sirens, but the man was gone.

Levi left Shooters without saying a word when he saw my text. He showed up as I was making my statement. The police tried to block him from entering, and he told them he lived here, and the victim was his girlfriend, so they let him by.

After giving my statement, Levi approached me and hugged me as I cried.

"It was him again, I think he's definitely my stalker," I continued. "It was pitch black in my room, and I was asleep. Then I woke up, and he slowly lowered my strap on my shoulder. Then, he started kissing my shoulder. Then, the next shoulder. I said your name, but you didn't answer. I grabbed my phone and turned on the flashlight and I saw him, again. I grabbed my pepper spray and sprayed him right in the face, and I got some in my face, too."

Levi said my face was bright red. I told him it burned, and I was coughing, and my eyes hurt. I told him how my stalker was having a hard time just trying to get out of my room. I called 911 while I texted you. I could tell Levi was pissed. He looked like he was about to go on a rampage, but I calmed him down. I'd never seen him so mad. I guess my stalker getting sexual with me was getting to him. How could it not?

The next day, I wanted to stay home, but I didn't want to be home alone ever again. If I had time off and no one else did, then I would just hang out at Shooters. I could play sand volleyball. I love volleyball. I worked another eight-hour shift docking boats, then had to race home and shower, get dolled up, and race back to Shooters 21 to be the hostess at the fine dining. I ensured one of my roommates had to do the same so I wouldn't be home alone.

I was wiped from the sun. But I was a great hostess. Levi was still bouncing at the nightclub. After work, I went to my car to leave, and I put my hand on the car door handle, but something behind the handle cut me. It was dark, and it was hard to see, so I used the flashlight on my phone and saw blood everywhere. I looked behind the handle, and a razor blade was taped to the inside of my handle with packing tape! I shined the light on my hand, and blood was streaming from the fleshy side of my fingers.

Oh my gosh, who the hell would do something like that?

It's him! I knew it was my stalker. I temporarily bandaged my hand with a spare shirt in my car and returned to Shooters for the first aid kit. I told my friend Wade, who worked at the bar, about what happened. He knew about my stalker. He asked if he did that and I told him I had no idea, but most likely.

After getting bandaged up, he walked me to my car. I drove to the emergency room to get stitches on my fingers. I had the razor blades and the tape in a little baggie. I'm fine with shedding a little blood for him to be finally caught. I knew this time we'd get him. Either prints from the tape or the blades. When the nurse asked how it happened, I told her. Then she said she was going to call the police.

When the police arrived, I told them what happened, and they took the baggy and said they would take it to forensics and dust for fingerprints on the razor blades I removed and the tape used to hold the blades to the underside of my door handle. I looked up, and I saw Levi. He came over and gave me a hug and kiss and he said Wade told him what happened, and I was going to the ER, so they found another bouncer so he could be with me. He's the best. "I can't believe that prick would do something like this." He said, "How bad is it?" he asked. I said, "well, I have more stitches than I can count. I got cut badly!" I replied. The Dr came in and gave me a tetanus shot, and I was on my way to getting discharged.

I got the news quickly, but it was another no-go. The police came and told me he must have been wearing gloves, because no prints showing up in their system. Figures, I thought to myself.

I obviously had to take the next day off because of my hand. I was actually home alone again, but it was daylight, and Steve and some friends were on their way down. I sat with pepper spray, waiting for them to show up. That, and Levi told me where his pistol was. At about 12 p.m., there was a knock at the door. I was hesitant to answer it. I looked out the window and saw a delivery truck, so I opened the door.

It was a flower delivery. But the bouquet had black roses mixed with blood-red roses, and in the center was a balloon that said, "Get well soon."

Who the hell are these from? I thought

I tipped the delivery man and read the note card in the envelope. It said, "I hope your hand heals quickly." "What?" I said out loud. No one knew except Wade and Levi. I hadn't even had a chance to tell my friends yet.

My stalker sent these; it had to be him. I was sure of it. It was definitely him with the black roses. No one I knew would send me black roses. He was escalating even more. I called the police again, and they came out and took the note for a handwriting sample. I told them they could have the flowers too. They were going to compare the handwriting from the $5 bill the other police had in evidence in Warrensburg.

Unfortunately, they learned the florist wrote the note. It was an online order, and he used a gift card purchased it with a stolen credit card.

DANG IT I screamed in my head.

I am so over this. If the cops couldn't catch him, then I would. I started thinking about all the traps I could make for him, to draw him out of hiding and apprehend him. This guy was good. Too good. It became apparent that I was not the first person he had stalked. I wonder what happened to the others.

When Levi finished his shift, he came to check on me before heading back for his second shift at the nightclub. He wanted this guy caught too, more specifically, wanting to kill this guy. He changed my bandage and grabbed the antibiotics I was prescribed. Levi refused to leave my side when I showed him the black and red roses and told him what the note said. He called in for his night shift. They were really cool about it. They knew what was going on. "Let's just chill at home tonight and enjoy ourselves," Levi said.

Levi was my mentor when all of this started, but now I am in love with him. I thought that we might even get married one day. I would be honored to be Mrs. Levi Beckett. Lord knows if he asked me tomorrow, I would say, YES! He has been so good to me. He has been my rock through all this from the beginning when I came to his gym for jujitsu. I was so happy he came to the lake with us.

I asked Levi about my plan to bait this guy and get him out of hiding. Then he, with his dad's gun, or the police, would be ready to get him. He said that that was too dangerous. There were better ways to catch him. We discussed some possibilities. But they all seemed unattainable.

Then we heard a loud 'boom' sound. It sounded like a gun going off. Levi grabbed his gun, looked out the window, and then went out front to investigate. I was biting my nails, waiting to see what it was. Levi came in and said that someone set off a firework, and then slashed all my tires, and his own tires. We called the cops, and they returned, took pictures, asked questions for a statement, and so on. This guy just wasn't going to stop.

Chapter 9: Levi attacked

It had been an amazing summer, even though I had to deal with the psycho stalker. But summer was quickly ending, and we needed to get back home to enroll in classes. We all put in our two-week notice, and we started packing

Mandi asked me if I wanted to be roommates for the school year. I told her yes, of course, that will be so fun. My bestie and I are in our own apartment. I figured she may not want to be my roommate with some psycho stalker on my heels, but she wasn't like that. I decided to stay local for my first two years of college. It was a lot less expensive, and I could go to the coast for my last two years if I still wanted to.

However, in my head, I still wanted to go to college out of state because of my stalker. But I have a feeling he will be caught soon. Or at least that is what I'm praying for. I looked at the scars on the back of my fingers from the razor blades he taped to my car door handle. I rubbed them as I remembered that day.

I also wanted to stay because I didn't want to leave Levi. I had a feeling if I did go to another college in another state during my last two years of school, he would come with me. He does so much for me I needed to do something for him. Maybe I already was, he was still around, and we were inseparable.

Classes started in two weeks. I started working back at Sonic, and Mandi decided to get a job there too. The money was just too good. We usually worked the same shifts but occasionally we had different shifts. We worked full-time until school started. We were both temporarily staying with our parents.

In the afternoon, before work, we went apartment hunting. We actually found an apartment with two bedrooms and one and a half baths. It was super clean and we seriously got lucky on this one! AND...It wasn't very expensive. We signed the lease on the spot.

We were going to move in the next day, Harry was actually ok with us taking off work. Our stuff was still in the U-Haul, which we rented, and parked it at Steve's house. Our apartment was on the other side of town from UCM where we went to school but that was no biggie. When we enrolled, we paid for parking spaces that were within walking distance to the campus.

Levi and some of his friends, along with Steve and his friends and my parents helped us move in. Our apartment was decorated with posters. Mandi's sister works at Blockbuster now, so we have a full wall-sized movie poster on the main wall. Typical I guess for poor college kids. We had a couch and futon. My parents found an old table for sale, and they refinished it and gave it to us. It was awesome, they did an really good job. Then we each had our own bedrooms. I had my full-size bed and desk with my laptop and school stuff scattered all over it.

On our first night in our apartment my car was broken into. A window had been blown out and I hadn't fully unpacked my car. My dad's expensive camera and several other items were in there. They were all gone. I called the police, and he was going through my car. I told him what was missing, and he wrote everything down. He said there was enough missing for this to be a felony if they found who did it.

He said fingerprints would be nearly impossible. And just left it at that. This didn't scream stalker to me. "Oh my gosh," I said loudly. "My cash, I had $600 cash in the glove box for our deposit and half the first month's rent," I said. I asked the officer there if I could open my glove box and check. He said he would. Then he pulled out the bank envelope. Whew, I let out a sigh. Thank God they didn't look in there. It wasn't locked or anything. Praise God! After a bit, Officer John was there. "Moved even farther south of town, huh?" He asked, laughing. "Yea, I couldn't pass up this apartment or the rent." He said he heard about the car break-in and figured he would come out and see if it was another stalker situation, or just random. We all thought it was just random, then the officer and Officer John left.

Levi stayed at our apartment almost every night. Same with Steve. Steve was a super nice and protective guy. He made Mandi so happy. We all became really good friends. And bonus; lots of people around to scare off the stalker.

Kaye and Misty both decided on other colleges out of state. Kaye was going to Florida and Misty was going to Pennsylvania. I will miss them so much. But we will keep in touch as much as we can.

Levi went back to teaching Jujitsu. It was amazing to spend the summer with him and my friends. We had a blast. This would be my first real year of college as a sophomore, because of my credits I earned going there while in high school. Even with the guys staying at our apartment a lot, I was still uneasy. So, I took things into my own hands.

I contacted someone from high school who had a reputation for illegal things. After finally tracking him down, I told him I needed a handgun. He said to meet him off Third and Pine Street in the alley tomorrow at 10 p.m. and bring cash. And I did. Pretty much all the cash I had. I told him I needed a compact handgun with as little recoil as possible in case I needed a quick second shot. I got the perfect handgun. My new gun was a Ruger 9mm. I named her Ruby. He sold me a few boxes of 9mm ammo. I felt like I was in some kind of movie; meeting a gun dealer in a dark alley. Like, really? This is what it's come to?

I wondered how Officer John would feel about a gun, seeing he had a problem with me carrying my knife. I had to laugh. I'll do whatever it takes to keep myself safe. I didn't tell anyone what I did. Not even Levi. It had to be done. I was 17 so I couldn't get one legally. And here I am a Criminal Justice major. If I got caught, I could kiss that career goodbye. But, for my safety, it was worth it. Yes, I was getting really good at Jiujitsu, but if Mr. Stalker had a gun, that wouldn't have done me much good. I need Levi to teach me how to disarm an assailant next, I thought.

Classes were a bit harder this semester. I signed up for Speech class but had to drop it my second day. My fear of public speaking was just too bad right now. I know I needed it to graduate, but I figured maybe next year. I gave a speech in high school once and ended up running from the class and throwing up because of my nerves. Public speaking was not my jam, even though I could strike up a conversation with pretty much anyone, and I was very social. The classroom was just not that kind of environment. I'm sure everyone was just as nervous as me, but maybe not. I replaced that class with Ancient Art.

I was in Health class, and I knew a guy from all the partying I did before we went to the lake. His name was Jeff. The professor asked if everyone in the room was 18 or older, before showing us graphic STD pictures. He raised his hand and pointed right at me and said, "her, she's still 17." Oh, I could have killed him. I was so embarrassed. "Well," she said, "If you are mature enough to be in college this won't kill you." I just smiled. I could feel my face turning red.

Mandi and I had English together, and also Chemistry. She was going into nursing, and I was getting a double major in Criminal Justice and Psychology. We planned a night out at the bowling alley, the four of us. This time, I wasn't looking at cute guys. I would have the hottest guy there, and he was my boyfriend and the sweetest boyfriend there was. I got hit on a few times by some Airmen who had too much to drink. Mandi did, too. Levi and Steve were chill. As long as they weren't harassing us, they didn't care. Plus, they saw their faces when we returned to them. I giggled under my breath. They were so laid back. I wasn't used to that. I liked it. Tommy was a total psycho and would have started a fight. Jaden wouldn't have cared because he would have been drunk.

I hadn't seen or had any weird stalker stuff happen for a bit. I just assumed he probably followed me and knew where my apartment was. Maybe not. Maybe I should also get a new car, so he won't know it's me.

Shortly after starting classes, I turned 18! Finally!! I could buy my own cigarettes instead of asking my friends to. I really should just quit, but now was definitely not the time. Not with all the stalker stuff going on. I was an adult. Legally and mentally. Kaye and Misty, who were back in town for the week, took me to Applebee's for my birthday. I drove. Misty was 21, so I figured I'd be the designated driver.

I had to use the ladies' room, and while I was in the bathroom sirens started going off for a tornado. I quickly finished my business and went back to our table. The girls said to follow them back to the bathrooms. That's where we were to take shelter, our waitress said. So, all the females were crammed into the tiny two-stall restroom, and we waited for the sirens to stop. The men went into the men's room. Finally, the sirens stopped, and we were in the clear.

We left the bathroom after washing our hands and finished eating our cold dinner. The manager approached every table and said that dinner was on the house. Nice, I thought. And it is probably less expensive than re-making everyone's food.

Then while we were getting ready to leave, I had a cyst on my ovary, and it burst. The pain was horrendous! They carried me to the car, and as we drove to another friend's house of Misty's, another tornado alarm started going off. I was laid out in the backseat, and they were trying to help me get into the house, so I told them to just leave me there. They wouldn't.

Just then, Levi and Steve showed up, and Levi carried me into the house. Everyone inside was looking at me funny. I was so embarrassed. There were so many people there that I didn't know, and I was dying in pain. Levi took my hand and helped me breathe through it. It lasted about 30 minutes. Then suddenly the pain was gone.

I got cysts on my ovaries all the time but had only had one burst before this one. The pain is unbearable.

We stayed at the house for a bit. Levi and I were doing our own thing and not socializing. We were busy talking and making out.

After about an hour, I dropped Misty off and then Mandi and I continued to our apartment. I was exhausted.

Levi stayed over again that night. Before bed, he wished me a happy birthday again and asked if I got his flowers. I told him no. So, I asked a couple of our apartment neighbors if they maybe got them by accident, and no one did. Levi apologized, but I told him it wasn't his fault. Thank you for the flowers.

The next day, I woke up and Levi had already left for the gym. I decided to get the apartment clean before the next week of classes and work. I took the trash to the dumpster and saw a 1-800 flower box. Intrigued, I pulled it out of the dumpster and opened it. They were my favorite flowers, Lilies, and there was a card. It read, "Happy birthday to the most beautiful woman I've ever laid eyes on. I love you." and Levi signed it. Who would have thrown my flowers in the trash!! I took them upstairs to my apartment, put them in a vase, and called Levi to tell him I had them. He didn't answer so I left him a message and told him they were in our apartment complex dumpster.

I wonder if my stalker did that. I decided to call Officer John just so he could add it to his notes, in case it was my stalker. Then I finished cleaning and ran a bunch of errands. The day flew by. I decided I'd turn in for the night. I needed some sleep, badly. I hadn't heard from Levi, so I texted him that I loved him and see him tomorrow.

The next day was the same as usual. Get up, get ready, go to school, go to work, come home, snack on something, and study. Day after day. Don't get me wrong, I loved being a college student. I was having a blast. We had fun parties too, so we did get some play in there on the weekends, and sometimes the weeknights. Our apartment would be packed! It kind of reminded me of the lake, but it was more laid back. Mandi and I wanted to have friends over for a small get-together party that next Saturday. I called Levi to let him know. Still no answer. I left him a voicemail and I texted him.

I hadn't heard from him in two days. It is so weird he wouldn't answer my calls, especially with this stalker around. I called again, and a strange voice answered the phone. I asked who it was, and he responded that he was Sergeant Harper, with the police department. He informed me that Levi had been stabbed in the parking lot of his gym, and his cell phone was in his evidence bag. The officer could hear the multiple calls, so he decided to answer. "How is Levi?" I asked. He said he was in the hospital in the ICU.

NO!! I screamed in my head.

I know what happened. It was my stalker. He must have felt threatened by my relationship with Levi.

Oh, Levi, I'm so sorry, I said to myself.

I bawled my eyes out after I hung up the phone. Mandi came running in and said, "Mac, what happened?" I told her that Levi was stabbed and was in the ICU, most likely from my stalker. I grabbed my keys, but Mandi said, "No, I'm driving." And we raced off to the hospital.

I cried and cried while Mandi drove. "Levi. I'm so sorry." I kept repeating.

I loved him so much. "It's my fault he's in ICU," I said. Mandi shot me down really quick. She said that Levi was doing exactly what he wanted to be doing: being with you. I asked Mandi if she knew that I thought we might get married one day. I loved him so much. She said she knew. I didn't know what to do with myself. I made sure the police knew that I had a severe stalker and that he was most likely the attempted murderer. I gave them the numbers of the officers I was working with here and told them to call Officer John, who was leading my case.

I went up to the ICU floor, and luckily, they allowed non-family members to visit. I sat with him and kissed his forehead and his hand. I begged him to wake up. I told him I loved him, and he would be ok. I even brought some of his favorite books to read to him. He loved reading about history and the Bible. They said talking and reading to him might help him wake up faster, so that's what I did. They said he might be able to hear what's going on.

I had been there four days now, since I first heard Levi was in the ICU. But he was in the ICU for six days in total. Mandi brought me fresh clothes and snacks. The hospital let me shower in the employee shower room. They were so sweet and thoughtful. His parents came every day to talk with him and give me a bit of a break. Then, while I was sleeping on his stomach after reading boring history for about an hour. I was exhausted. Then, I felt a hand brush through my hair. I perked straight up and said his name. He was really dizzy, but he was muttering something I couldn't understand. After his third try, he said, "I love you." "Oh Levi, I love you too. So much!" I told him. Then I told him I would get a doctor, and I'd be right back. "Try not to talk," I said before I opened the door. I opened his door and yelled, "I need a doctor! Levi is awake!" Then I went to sit back down by him, his parents right behind me.

Nurses and the Doctor were on the way! When they got there, they asked us to leave the room, and they tended to Levi. I paced the hall and peered in the window to his room.

What was going on? I thought.

They finally came out, and I asked them if he was going to be okay. They said yes, but he lost a lot of blood and needed to take it easy. The dagger missed all his major internal organs.

His 'dagger,' It was my stalker!.

They said I could go back in and visit him. After a nod from his parents, I went by his side and sat with him, holding his hand. He said he loved me again and thanked me for reading to him. I was shocked. He did know what was going on! I told him I loved him too, so much. I didn't know what I would do without him. Then he said, "I saw him."

"What?" I said.

"Your stalker, I saw him. He fits your sketch perfectly. I saw him right after he stabbed me from behind, he told me that you belonged to him, and he doesn't share."

I didn't know what to say. "Levi, I'm so sorry this happened to you because of me."

He said he'd take a bullet for me any day, or in this case, a dagger through the abdomen. Then he tried to laugh, but it hurt too much.

I said, "Did I tell you I love you, Levi? I mean, I am in love with you. You scared me so much. I can't imagine my life without you."

"Yes," he said, "except the 'in love with me' part, can you say that again."

"I am madly in love with you, Levi," I said with a giant smile.

He smiled and said, "I am completely and utterly in love with you, Mac."

I wept. I was so happy he was going to be ok. And I would be there for his recovery every step of the way.

The police showed up to ask Levi questions and had him describe the assailant with a sketch artist to sketch his attacker, basically what my stalker looked like. Levi gave a great description, matching my sketch, but his sketch was better.

I took a picture of the sketch, not that I'd ever forget it. But it was good to have handy. He looked to be in his late 20s. He actually looked a little familiar to me. He was clean shaven and had a long face and light brown hair. His blue eyes looked full of hatred, and you could see the crazy in them. He kind of looked like Tommy.

But I know it wasn't him. He wasn't capable of all this. Besides, when I broke it off, he cried and then avoided me like the plague. And the car, it wasn't what he drove. I wish I still had a picture of Tommy on my phone to show Levi. I checked my deleted pictures, but they had already gone past the 30 days and were gone forever.

Should I tell the police he resembled Tommy? I thought.

I asked Levi what he thought, and he said definitely if I see any resemblance, I should tell the police so they could question him.

I went after the police before they left the building and gave them the information on Tommy. Where he lived, the last time I contacted him and any other information they asked for. Then, I rushed back to the ICU to be with Levi.

Things were getting hard. I was drained, scared, and running low on energy, and my parents were very worried about me. They begged me to move home. After losing one of my jobs, bills, tuition, and books, I decided to move back home. It was my parents' idea, and they made some good points as to why it would be beneficial. I also didn't want to put Mandi in danger. Mandi was totally good with my decision. So, reluctantly, I moved back into my parent's house. Mandi's boyfriend, his friends, Levi's friends, and my parents helped me pack up and move.

Mandi and Steve decided to keep the apartment we were living in and live together. Levi was still living at home, so he was good. As soon as he recovered, he'd be home and have help during his recovery. With me too, of course. I hated quitting school and moving home but my safety was seriously at risk. And possibly anyone I cared about as well. I also wanted to help Levi in his recovery. That was the least I could do after all he had done for me. And I did. I was at his house, drove him to his physical therapy appointments, and stayed there with him, cheering him on while he was gaining back his strength.

My parents still had the security system in place. Patrol cars randomly drove past our house or sat outside our house for a while. My mom brought them drinks and snacks and thanked them for keeping us safe. I was scared for everyone I cared about. No one knew I had a gun. I hadn't told anyone. I was going to tell Levi, but that's when he got stabbed. I slept with my gun. I was good at concealing it.

Levi was nearly done with recovery and physical therapy. He was recovering very quickly. Praise God. I just prayed that my stalker wouldn't try to finish the job. He must know that law enforcement and all of us knew what he looked like by now. Which brought me to my next thought. Now that he knows we know what he looks like... will he go ahead and try to end this show?

I had a sit down with Officer John. I asked how he thought things were going to go now that Levi had survived, and we knew what he looked like. I asked if they had questioned Tommy and how that went. He told me he wasn't driving the car that was following me, and he acted as if he had no idea what they were talking about. He said he wanted nothing more to do with me and wouldn't care if I was with someone else.

I wasn't sure I was buying it. His car may not have been there when he showed up. Maybe he got a new car, or perhaps he was borrowing another car. But maybe I just wanted it to be him so this would be over. But Officer John didn't think he was our guy.

Dang it, I screamed in my head.

So, this isn't over. Officer John told me that moving home was a good idea, and he was glad I did. Also, taking a break from school. He said I might want to take a break from Levi, too.

"Heck NO," I said. It just came out of my mouth before I knew I was going to say it. I was not letting this guy keep me from the love of my life. I would understand if Levi wanted a break, but he didn't. So that was out of the question. I told him I was still carrying pepper spray and my knife. I definitely didn't tell him about the gun. Then I'd be in jail.

"I guess I'd be safe there, I laughed. He warned me again that, most likely, he would come after me next. In the scheme of things and his patterns, I'm next.

I'm next?! I replayed his words in my head.

Now that they had another description, he would end this and move on to someone else, probably in another town or even state. He is probably searching for his next target right now.

I went to the mall to find a gift for Levi. I searched several stores trying to find an awesome top. I had to use the restroom, so I headed down the sloped floor and into the corridor and the ladies' room was on the right. I went in the stall and did my business. I was washing my hands and I looked up in the mirror to check my makeup. I froze. My stalker was behind me. As I was about to scream, he put his hand over my mouth and dragged me into a stall. He put a dagger to my throat and removed his hand from my mouth. I didn't dare make a sound. Then he reached down between my legs and touched me there. I wanted to scream so bad but I couldn't move with a dagger on my throat. After assaulting me, he tried to kiss me but I turned my head, and I felt the blade cut into my skin on my neck. Another lady entered the bathroom and I screamed! She immediately went to our stall and she said she was calling the police. My stalker opened the door and fled from the ladies' room. I just stood there and cried. I called Levi while I waited on the police. Once they were there, I gave my statement, and so did the witness that called the police. She was so nice and comforting to me. Then I left the mall, with out a gift, and drove to Levi's. He gave me a huge hug, and said that I shouldn't go anywhere alone. He is probably near the "tying up loose ends" portion of the stalking.

He had to be stopped. If I didn't, who would? I don't want him to find a new target. I don't want anyone to go through what I'm going through and have been going through. I was nervous about using my gun, so I went to an open outdoor range and shot off a clip of ammo. I needed to get used to it. It was far easier than I thought it would be. I wore a cap and sunglasses, trying to hide that I was not old enough to have a gun. I went to the range several times until I was nearly out of ammo. I felt comfortable with my gun and felt confident that I could use it on my stalker if needed. I wanted to kill him. I wanted him dead after what he did to Jaden, and now Levi, and myself, of course. He was tainting all the good things in my life. Like dancing with Levi, Levi stopped kissing my shoulders, which I loved. But I'm glad he did, and I didn't have to ask because it bothered me now, all because of this damn stalker.

I had told Levi that I bought the gun in some alley, and he wasn't shocked at all. Being he brought a pistol to the lake, he couldn't blame me for wanting a gun. He was just glad I didn't get caught. I told him I only had two clips of ammo left, so I needed to call that guy again to see if we could get more ammo. Levi said not to risk it again. He had plenty of 9mm that I could have.

Awesome, I thought.

I told him how badly I wanted to kill him, and Levi said to me if it had to happen, it had to happen, but we should be wanting the police to get him. Having that much hatred would kill my innocent and beautiful soul. Levi is so sweet. And he was right. I didn't want to take a life. If someone else did, I'd be okay with that. Put this monster down like a dog.

Chapter 10: Nobody's Prey

I was missing living alone, but it was safer, I guess, at home. My parents were cool about letting Levi stay the night here and there, on the couch. I still hadn't told my parents I had a gun. I don't think that would go over well. I was working full-time at Sonic since I wasn't going to school. I worked a lot with Mandi, which was awesome. I had been stalked for over a year now.

I knew my stalker was looking for his new victim, and I shuddered at the thought of some other young girl going through this. According to the police, he was probably about done with me, and I needed to be extra cautious at work, coming home, and keeping the doors locked and the alarm on. They said they would keep the police presence around our house off and on throughout the day.

I turned the corner on my street and saw a patrol car there. I rolled down the window to thank him, and he said he was about to leave, and be sure to lock up. I said, "Yes Sir." and saluted him. We both laughed. I got home and parked in the garage. I closed the garage door in case he tried to slip in before I got out. That's why my parents were making me park in the garage. Also, so my stalker wouldn't know whether I was home or not. It was safer. Our garage door didn't have windows, and blinds covered the one garage window. I went to open my car door, but the garage light was out. I guess it needed a new bulb. The hair on the back of my neck rose. Something felt off, I froze, I couldn't move. I was stuck, and my heart was beating so fast. The eerie feeling wasn't passing, but I told myself everything was fine. But it wasn't.

He's here

As I reached for my car handle, I saw a figure on the stairs in the garage. I quickly locked all the car doors. I tried to open the garage door to pull out, but he must have locked it. I started blowing my horn to alert anyone in earshot. I threw the car in reverse and floored it. All that did was dent the garage door. He just stood there staring at me, then laughing.

He slowly walked over to my window with one of those window-breaking devices in his hand, and with minimal effort, it busted the glass of my driver's window. He reached in and manually unlocked the door and opened it. I went for my pistol, but he pulled me out of my car by my hair.

Shit

I screamed in my head. *My gun!*

Then he said, "You'll never learn, so I'm going to teach you a lesson."

His voice sounded familiar. There was the faintest light in the garage through the window, even with the blinds pulled. It was coming from the streetlight. It was him. The man who danced with me, kissed my shoulders, roofied me, yes, that is definitely him, the weirdo from the bar! It's been him all along? I asked myself in disbelief. The man in the sketch Levi and I gave it was definitely him. It was his eyes. Crazed.

Once out of the car, he started dragging me into the house. When he opened the door, the alarm started screaming. He had his arm around my neck from behind. I grabbed it and flipped him over onto the floor.

Thank you, jujutsu, I thought.

I ran towards the front door, and he extended his leg and tripped me. I fell flat on my face. He grabbed me by my hair again and took me to the alarm panel, and then I felt it. He stabbed me from behind. He put the bloody dagger to my neck and made me disarm the alarm.

Crap, what is the panic code! I totally blanked.

I was in so much pain, and my gun was in my purse in the car. I punched in the four digit code, disarming it, and then he threw me to the ground. I winced in pain.

Help Me! Please, somebody, Help!

I wanted to scream, but I couldn't. I looked down at my abdomen and saw all the blood, it was running down my shirt and my jeans. I needed something to stop the bleeding. I could taste the blood in my mouth.

I'm going to die, right here and now, I thought while I tried to stop the bleeding.

I looked up at him, and he was smiling, thoroughly enjoying watching me die. He was toying with the dagger. Probably the same one that killed Jaden and almost killed Levi. He just wanted to watch the end of the show. The end of my life. Everything that he's done started racing through my head. Every act to get my attention. I'm trying to figure out why. Why me? What did I do to this guy for this to happen?

I'm not going to let this psycho get any further gratification, and I tried to run. It was more like a speed walk, but he followed me. Then he smugly said, "Where do you think you are going, Mac?" as he stalked me like I was his prey, with the dagger in his hand, ready to slaughter me.

I'm nobody's prey, I told myself.

I immediately went into survival mode. I was trying to get somewhere where there was a weapon of some kind without him seeing me grab it. I grabbed a towel off the kitchen counter of our farmhouse-decorated kitchen. It was my mom's favorite towel with cows and milk canteens patterned all over it. I took the towel and pushed it hard on my abdomen. It slowed down some of the bleeding, but not all. I turned the corner from our kitchen to the dining room. I was in such a haze, and I could barely see straight. *My dad's gun*, I thought. He keeps it loaded in the lower drawer of the coffee table. I had to get to it, I now only focused on getting to the coffee table.

I was starting to get light-headed, but I fought it. I pretended to fall to the ground so I could crawl, I needed to be low to the ground to get to my dad's gun. Then he kicked me from behind, and I was laid out on the carpet. I cried out in pain, but I had to get back up and crawl around the side of the coffee table because that's where my dad's gun was.

Please be unlocked, I begged God. The drawer must be unlocked, or I'm going to die.

I just had to stay conscious. His dagger isn't going to win against my gun. I wasn't very confident in my aim under these conditions but hitting him at least once would put us on equal ground.

The way he looked at me was so evil. He cocked his head from side to side like a dog and went from having a puzzled face to a face full of enjoyment. He smiled and said, "Your life is in my hands, Mac. How does that feel?"

I just ignored him, which pissed him off. He kicked me in the stomach, I screamed!

"How does that feel?" He repeated.

"It feels awesome!" I replied sarcastically.

Then he grabbed me by my hair again and threw my head down.

OK, Mac, quit pissing him off.

I had to stay focused. If I can't get that gun, my life will be over.

I thought of my parents, Levi, my amazing boyfriend, my sister, and my bestie, Mandi. Their faces flooded my mind. I needed to survive. For them. I prayed to God that I could hit him with every shot! I was there….now was the time….this would be life or death. I reached for the handle on the drawer and pulled it.

Damn it!

It was locked. My gun was still in my purse in my car. Why didn't I grab it when I first saw him, I thought. I couldn't crawl anymore. He straddled me while I was lying flat on my stomach on the carpet in my living room. He turned me over. He said we were going to a little fun, then go on a little ride.

FUN? What did that mean? And a ride? Was he abducting me? He took his dagger and cut my shirt open, exposing my bra and abdomen.

NO! I thought. He's going to rape me.

"Do you remember me?" He asked.

"No." I lied.

"Well, that's too bad." He said.

"I'm the one who roofied you at the bar. We had a connection at the bar, remember?" He asked.

I again answered, "No, I don't remember you at all."

I just wanted to piss him off.

"It must be the roofie that is affecting your memory." He said. Then I said, "I just remember some loser hitting on me when I just wanted to get water from the bar."

That really pissed him off. He put both his hands around my neck and started choking me. He quickly quit. "I'll hold off on that until after," he said.

I put pressure on my abdomen and then tried to buck him off me, as I learned in jiujitsu. But I was too weak, and it hurt too much. I started crying. Then I tried to buck him off again while putting a ton of pressure on my wound, and it worked. I knocked him onto the coffee table, and I tried to get up and crawl away. He laughed, dragging me back, turned me over and started to straddle me again, this time digging his knee into my side, where he stabbed me. I screamed out in pain. He stood up to unzip his pants, but I kicked him between the legs as hard as I could, launching him backward across the room and into my mom's curio cabinet. I heard him cry out in pain. This was not how I was going to lose my virginity.

"Stupid Bitch!" he screamed at me.

He was pissed. He came back and slapped me. He pulled zip ties out of his pocket. I couldn't stand the thought of being tied up and helpless, so I fought him as much as I could. He screamed to hold still, or he'd stab me again. I was on the losing end of this. He finally got my hands zip tied, then he zip tied my hands to the coffee table leg. I could barely move; this was happening, and there was nothing I could do. Or was there?

"Do you want me to kiss your shoulders again, I know how much you liked it last time." he said, "I heard you moan." He bragged. "Did I turn you on?" he asked, then answered his own question, "I know I did," he said.

I said, "no, you actually made me throw up a little in my mouth."

Then he said, "I'm pretty sure you liked it."

I rolled my eyes. Then he smacked me, and hard. He forced my legs apart and laid down on me. He put the dagger up to my throat, "I'll put this away if you promise to behave," he said.

I said I'd behave. I was losing so much blood and was having a hard time breathing. Then I heard the zipper on his pants. I was going in and out from the blood loss. "I'm going to need you to stay awake for this, Mac," he said as he unbuttoned and unzipped my black uniform pants. Then he started pulling my pants and my panties down. He got them past my hips.

This was not happening; I screamed in my head.

He took the dagger and cut open my bra, and he touched my breasts. I was disgusted. I'm sure he could see it on my face, and I was happy.

Levi had taught me another way to get out of zip ties if you know you will be zip tied. First, I made sure when he zip tied my hands, I had wiggle room by making it look tight by making my hands look like they were as close together as possible while I was getting zip tied. And I did. But not enough to get out of them.

He was in such a hurry he didn't look too hard. I started to try and wiggle free. As my stalker was about to rape me, I screamed as loud as my injuries would allow. He said laughing, "no one is coming, and no one will hear you, so just lay back and enjoy being with a real man, Mac."

I wanted to vomit again.

I screamed at him, "you are nowhere near a real man. You are a coward who has to force sex on women."

That got me slapped again. Then he took the dagger and stabbed me again in the chest. I screamed.

"Why don't you keep your mouth shut." he yelled. "You are mine. Never forget that." He said. "I can do whatever I want to you, you belong to me."

I was having trouble breathing.

"Looks like we aren't going on that little ride now. I don't think you will survive it. At least I can screw you before you bleed out," he said. "Virgins are the best. I can't wait. I bet you can't either."

I didn't bother to reply.

I was not going to let him rape me. I just needed to figure out how. He wanted me awake and to look at him. So, I pretended to pass out. He cut my abdomen with the dagger, thinking that it would wake me up, but I put on my best poker face and didn't move or make a noise, even though it hurt like hell.

Then he pulled out a syringe and injected me with God knows what, but I was wide awake but groggy at the same time. "I told you I want you awake for this, Mac," he said.

He pulled my pants and panties down to my ankles. He spread my bent legs and laid on top of me. I was in so much pain and about to have a panic attack from whatever he injected me with. I tried bucking him off again, and he said, "I'm going to need you to lay still," and then he slapped me again.

I screamed in pain. Then I pretended to pass out. He smacked me again, and I put on my best poker face again and didn't make a sound or facial expression, just like the last time, and that was hard. I seriously deserved an Oscar for that one.

Suddenly, a large garden paver flew through the glass of the back sliding door, right where we were.

Who did that? I asked myself.

Then I saw Levi, and he immediately went into action, kicking my stalker in the head, then put him in a choke hold and pulled him off me. I couldn't wiggle my way out of the zip ties, a little blood was involved, but I wasn't free. I needed to lift the coffee table just a little to slide the zip ties off the leg. I was running on pure adrenaline at this point. So I rolled over and lifted up the coffee table with my knee, as much as I could. Then, I slipped the zip ties off the leg of the coffee table. My arms were free, but my hands were still bound. Sitting up was excruciating, but I had to pull my pants up. I pulled them up as much as I could with my hands bound, I got my panties almost up but not my pants because I had to lay back down. I was about to pass out. I just laid there, completely exposed.

Levi and my stalker wrestled. I heard glass breaking, I heard punches, and I heard what sounded like a bone snap. I was trying to stay conscious, but it was so hard. I lost way too much blood. I grabbed the blood-soaked towel from the kitchen and re-applied it to my abdomen, and put as much pressure as I could on my new wound. Then I saw the dagger on the ground. I was going to try and go for it, but Levi saw it too and kicked it hard. It went flying into the kitchen. Levi put him in another choke hold and in less than 30 seconds, my stalker slumped over and fell to the ground. He was out cold.

I pulled the cabinet drawer again; I needed that gun. Then, one last ditch effort, I pulled as hard as I could and wiggled the handle around a bit, and it opened! It wasn't locked, just jammed, and I was too weak to pull it open.

Levi came over to me and applied pressure to both my wounds as he cradled his cell phone with his shoulder, and he called 911. Then he put it on speaker to keep pressure on my wounds.

Then, over Levi's shoulder, I saw my stalker get up. He was going for his dagger, and I grabbed the gun. Levi saw me pull the gun, and he moved to the side. I shot three rounds at him. I hit him once in the chest. He slumped down to the ground but got up quickly, turned around, and ran out the front door, leaving his dagger behind.

Levi started to go after him but then stopped because I needed medical attention. "Mac, it's Levi. You are going to be OK, do you hear me?" Levi said. "I love you so much." He told me.

"Thank you for loving me and showing me what real love is," I told him.

"I love you so much. I wanted to marry you. Please tell my parents and my loved ones that I love them too," I continued as I was saying goodbye.

"Mac, don't talk like that. Fight!" he said.

Fight, I must fight.

He put a ton of pressure on both my stab wounds. I cried out in pain. Levi said he was sorry, but he had to put pressure on my wounds. My face hurt too from my stalker smacking me around, but it didn't compare to the stab wounds. "What did that bastard do to you, babe?" He could see the bruises, the cut on my abdomen, and the bumps on my face. I didn't have the energy to answer. I just stared at the ceiling, trying to keep my eyes open and breathe. I couldn't talk anymore because I was so out of breath. I didn't even care that I was practically naked anymore. I knew I was dying.

After fighting to stay awake, about five minutes later, I heard the sirens. The police, fire department, and ambulance were all there. When they came in, Levi said to the cops, "He's been shot, and his car with the dent is parked two streets over, go after him. Maybe the shot to the chest slowed him down!"

Then, several officers were out the door, heading towards where Levi said his car was. The paramedics took over for Levi, and Levi told the police everything while the paramedics worked on me. Levi told the police that I shot at him three times and hit him once in the chest. He said he broke his middle right finger in the struggle.

"We need to get her to a trauma hospital now, or she's not going to make it," the paramedic interrupted. The paramedics put a blanket over me, covering my open chest my breasts, and my hips. That made me feel so much better. They were getting me on a stretcher for the ambulance just as forensics arrived. Levi showed them where the dagger was.

I couldn't keep my eyes open any longer. I heard Levi ask if he could ride with me in the ambulance, but Officer John said no because they needed his statement and to ask him more questions. "Can't it wait?" he asked. Officer John paused for a minute. "Yes, it can wait. Ride with Mac to the hospital." "Thank you," Levi said.

I could barely talk but weakly said, "I love you, Levi." On the way out my front door on the stretcher, I asked Levi, "did they get him?" But before he could answer, I passed out from blood loss.

Chapter 11: ICU

I woke up in the hospital. I immediately went into panic mode.

Where was I? What happened? Did they catch him? Am I safe?

Then I saw Levi. My eyes closed again, but I forced them open.

Levi was asleep on one of the chairs. I tried to call out to him, but I had something down my throat, and it hurt to try and make any sound. Since I couldn't talk, I knocked over a water bottle that was near my hand, and Levi woke up.

He saw my eyes were open and he was beside me in seconds. Then my eyes closed again, and I couldn't open them.

"Fight it, Mac," he said, "keep your eyes open, come back to us." He begged.

I tried to speak again. He kissed my forehead and told me not to talk. He was going to call for a doctor.

This felt familiar. I had done the same for him, I thought.

I was still in panic mode. I didn't know what happened with my stalker or what happened after I passed out. The doctors came in and asked Levi to leave while they evaluated my condition. They gave me a sedative to calm me down. Then, they pulled me off the ventilator to see if I could breathe on my own. Thankfully, I could, so they didn't need to put it in again.

I heard the doctor tell the nurse that they needed to do some imaging to make sure my lung would hold up. I wondered what the tube was for and why I couldn't breathe. I was too out of it to ask. They knew I was awake, but out of it.

I was in and out as they did all their tests. Then, I was able to open my eyes again and keep them open. The doctor told me to stay calm. He gave me some water. My throat was dry and scratchy. He said he was Doctor Heller, he looked like he was my age. He had red hair and caring eyes. He said he was the main doctor in my case and performed my surgery.

Surgery? I thought.

Then the doctor told me the stab to my chest collapsed one of my lungs, and that was why I was on a ventilator.

"You were very lucky with that stab," He said. "You are lucky to be alive, you coded on us twice," the doctor informed me. He told me they have had a police officer at my door since I had arrived, and he was going to stay until I was released, so I had nothing to be afraid of. I was safe and in good hands. The doctor then told me that I had been given a blood transfusion as well. I was out for eight days, he told me.

Eight days! I said in my head.

He said they put me in a medically induced coma for two days so my body could heal, then they stopped the coma medication and were waiting for me to wake up for six days. He said I sure took my time, and he grinned. "I'm so happy to have you back with us, Makayla."

He said I needed to have limited visitors, only one at a time, and the police were going to talk to me when I was ready so I could tell them what happened. He also gave me something to help my throat so I could speak without so much pain from being on the ventilator.

I nodded my head and asked for some more water, and to see Levi in a groggy voice. They said they would send him in. I vaguely remember some visitors and my hand being held while I was out. I felt like I was paralyzed in a shell. It's so hard to explain.

The doctor said he called my parents and let them know I was awake. They were on the way. I nodded again. I wanted to see them so much. I had a whole list of visitors that came. My parents, my sister, Mandi and Steve, and of course Levi, and several other people. They didn't think I was going to survive my injuries.

Did I kill him, or did they catch him? That was all I wanted to know.

After Levi came in, I asked him if he was dead. He said, "No, he got away. You were able to slow him down, though. You hit him once in the chest. And in the struggle, I broke his middle finger on his right hand."

Officer John came in first. It was nice to see a friendly face. He said he wasn't there for my statement. He just wanted to see how I was doing. He said he'd get my statement tomorrow, when I could talk without pain. But I didn't care about the pain, I wanted to tell him everything now so they could catch him.

I told him, "I'm ready to tell you everything," I said. "He was waiting for me in the garage, and he stabbed me, and forced me to disarm the alarm. Then followed me around, just watching me like I was his prey."

I'm nobody's prey. I thought to myself again.

I continued on, I told them how I was trying to get to my dad's gun, that's why I was crawling around. I told them how he was about to rape me, and I kicked him between the legs, and it hurt. Then he stabbed me again because of it. I told them that when he was about to rape me, and he told me afterwards we were going for a little ride. Then after the second stab, he said we may not be going on that ride after all. He didn't think I'd survive the trip. Then, right when he was ready to rape me, Levi showed up. I could hear his zipper in my head as I told the story. I told them Levi threw a paver through the glass sliding back doors.

They said in Levi's statement, he came by and saw the stalker's car down the street, and when he got to the door, he heard you screaming so he picked up a paver and broke the back glass door. I told him that was correct. The alarm never went off because my stalker forced me to disarm it after he stabbed me and then held the dagger to my throat. I forgot what the panic code number was, so I just had to turn it off, I explained to Officer John. I told him I got my dad's gun and shot three times, hitting him in the chest once. I told him I saw him collapse, but he got up, turned around, and ran out the front door. I asked if they recovered his dagger. He told me they did, and it was the same weapon used to kill Jaden, and stab Levi. Some of Jaden's DNA was still on the blade, along with Levi's, under the handle. And now my blood was on it too.

They found Jaden's killer! I was relieved to hear that, but also saddened because he died because of me. The police suspected he was jealous, and that was probably why he killed Jaden and tried to kill Levi.

I remembered every detail that I was conscious for anyway.

I started to tear up again. I told Officer John that I think I knew who he was now, more like where I had seen him before all this started. I told him I thought he was the guy at the bar who kept flirting with me and how I kept blowing him off. My stalker himself reminded me that we met at the bar, and we were flirting, which we were not. I was just waiting for my water but had to go to the ladies' room. He drugged my water while I was in the ladies' room, and tried to take me home, but Mandi and Misty saw what was going on and stopped him. They took me to the hospital, and they did blood work, and I was in fact, drugged.

I was relieved to know where I had met the guy, and why all this was happening. Maybe not "why" exactly, but I could draw some conclusions. It was him all along. He's been trying to get my attention since that night he drugged me. It's pretty pathetic, really, and he obviously had some mental issues.

Why me? I wondered.

There were girls way prettier than me. Why did he pick me? Was I too nice to him? Did he think I was interested?

Officer John said they recovered a gun with the serial number filed off in my purse in my car. He asked me where I got it. I told him that I met some guy in an alley and bought one. I asked him, "can you blame me."

"No," he said. "I made sure the gun disappeared."

I gave him a questioning look.

He said, "I made sure it was sent in anonymously to the gun program where you could drop off your gun, no questions asked."

"Thank you so much," I said.

I asked if I was in trouble, and he said no. With a wink, he said he was sure it was just to protect myself. He told me to rest up and get better.

"OK," I said. "But is he really still out there, will he try again?" I asked him.

"It's hard to tell," he replied. "You hit him once in the chest like you said, but he hasn't shown up at any nearby hospitals, and they have to call the police for gunshot wounds." It's not over, Mac," he said with a saddened look on his face. I think he truly was feeling bad for me.

I was emotionally and physically a wreck. Officer John left, and told Levi he could go in. Levi was there at the ICU with me the entire time, like I was for him, he never left. And I could tell looking at him. His hair was disheveled, he looked exhausted and maybe even lost some weight. He had a small bag of clean clothes and showered in the employee showers just like I did. Most of the staff remembered him from when he was in the ICU. They took good care of him, and me. Levi's parents were the ones that brought him fresh clothes and told him to take care for me.

Oh good, they like me, I thought.

Levi started to tear up. He said he thought for sure I wasn't going to make it. My injuries were very severe, and I coded two times, one while he was there holding my hand, the second time while my parents were with me. "I watched you die, Mac," he said. It was horrible. I saw a tear roll down his cheek.

I told him the doctor told me that. I told him I was sorry I scared him, and I vaguely remembered him holding my hand. He said he read to me, too. My favorite books, self-help, inspirational, and motivational books, and of course the Bible. He read Psalms multiple times to me.

He said he was seriously about to hang himself reading my self-help books. They were so boring, and he laughed. "Plus, you are perfect the way you are, Mac," he told me and kissed my hand. There, I had to laugh, and it hurt.

I said, "It couldn't have been more boring than me reading your history books to you. I thought they might keep you unconscious longer." I laughed, and it hurt!

"Hey, history is important," he claimed.

"If you say so," I replied, smiling.

He saw me smiling and said that he wasn't sure he'd ever see my beautiful smile again. I blew him a kiss and told him I loved him.

One book we both had in common that we loved to read was the Bible. I told him I remembered him reading it, or parts of it. There were a few verses in Psalms that were my favorite that he read. I told him a few times I felt like I was awake but couldn't open my eyes. I couldn't move. It was like I was stuck in a shell, just like when I was starting to wake up. He said he had that feeling as well when he was in the ICU. "Now we have more stuff in common," I joked. He laughed, and I giggled…ouch.

"I would prefer for us to have other things in common, wouldn't you agree?" I asked, smiling.

"Yes, definitely," he said.

I told him, "I can feel how much you love me, just by how you touch me."

Then he said, "That's good, because I love you and I touched you a lot while you were out."

There was a knock at the door, and it was my parents. Just seeing their faces, I started to cry. Levi said he'd go to the waiting room so they could come in. I thanked him and he gave me a kiss. My mom, Krista, gave Levi a hug, and my dad, Derek, shook his hand. They came in, and I was still tearing up. They both gave me a very gentle hug and kiss. My mom sat down and held my hand while my dad stood behind her.

"Praise God you are OK, I've been praying nonstop," she said.

I told her and my dad, I loved them. I asked if they knew what all happened. They said just what Levi told them, but not what happened before he got there. I told them about the garage, the alarm, him stabbing me, and trying to get dad's gun.

My mom said, "Praise God Levi was able to get inside in time. Just before your stalker was about to rape you, she said and stared to cry.

I told them that he was right about to rape me, he had me nearly naked and zip tied to the coffee table leg, then my stalker said we were going for a little ride afterward, well, until he stabbed me again. Then he told me he didn't think I'd survive 'our little ride.'

My dad punched the beam next to the wall. "Dad," I said," stop, I'm OK."

He said he was sorry, but he thought I'd be safer at home. My mom said when she got home and saw all the blood in the kitchen and living room her mind went to the worst. "I thought that he killed you, Makayla, and took your body somewhere. There was so much blood. I thought for sure you were dead." She started crying.

I told them that must have been very scary for them.

My mom continued, "We called the police, and they told us what happened and that you were at the hospital in ICU."

Officer John had asked another officer to call them, but they never did. The police told them they were sorry that they came home to the mess without knowing what happened. My parents said they rushed straight to the hospital, and I had tubes and wires and IV lines all over me and one tube down my throat, and they were preparing me for emergency surgery, with the trauma team.

A nurse came in and checked my vitals. She looked at me and told me that my brother called to get an update on my condition, and he was in between flights on his way to see me.

"My brother?" I asked to clarify.

"Yes," she said.

"I don't have a brother." I told her.

"Oh my gosh," she said. "I'm so sorry, I gave him a complete update on your condition."

"It had to be my stalker." I said out loud. The nurse left quickly.

I called after her. "Please notify the staff that any updates on my condition must be done in person with my mom or dad's approval, or Levi's approval. "

She said OK and rushed out. I shook my head. My parents didn't react much to it. They were just relieved I was alive but after so many days of me not waking, they thought I wasn't coming back to them.

I told them how much I loved them both, and that I remember mom stroking my hand one of those days.

"You did?" she said excitedly.

"Yes." I said. "I just couldn't open my eyes. Or move. Then I was out again."

She said she knew I felt it because my hand moved, but everyone kept telling her it was just a natural spasm, that I wasn't awake, but I was!

"Did you hear that, Derek?" she asked my dad. My dad just smiled.

"You coded twice, Makayla," my mom said, "Once with Levi, and once with us. Watching you die was the worst experience of our lives. Praise God they were able to bring you back!."

"I know, the doctor told me. That's really scary to hear," I said.

She said, "For you and us and the posse of people in the waiting room!" You have so many people who love you, especially Levi," she said. "He's a stand-up gentleman. You had so many people in the waiting area. Just waiting to come in and talk to you. We all thought you were going to die. Even the doctors were preparing us for it. Officer John even came by on and off duty a few times to check in on you and see if there was any progress."

I felt so loved. I can't believe how many people have been here and come to talk to me and try to wake me up. It sounded like someone was always talking to me all day long.

My parents said they'd be right back, they wanted to hear from the doctor what comes next and if there was anything in particular they needed at home for when I was released, which would probably be another week. They both hugged and kissed me and promised they were coming right back.

I was alone, probably for the first time.

There were flowers, balloons, and a couple of teddy bears in my room. I just now noticed them. I was taking in the scene. As I scanned over the flowers, I couldn't help but wonder if there was going to be a black bouquet, or something from the stalker! My room had all kinds of medical equipment, a pole for my IV, I had heart monitoring wires all over my chest, stomach, and legs. I had some blankets on me and was in a hospital gown. The IV in my hand hurt. I had a pulse ox on my finger that was taped on, along with a blood pressure cuff that kept going on and off. It was so annoying. I'm shocked that that alone didn't wake me up. I was groggy, and my eyes were starting to get heavy. But I couldn't quit looking at the flowers and "get well soon" gifts and wondering if my stalker sent any of them.

Levi came back into the room. He saw me eyeing all the flowers, and balloons, and stuffed animals with a panicked face. He asked me what was wrong, and I explained to him why, so he went from flowers to flowers, to balloons, to bears, and read the notes and who they were from for each one. I felt so much better. I knew everyone who sent or brought the gifts.

He said, "I'm sorry, but none are from me. I couldn't leave your side."

"But guess what?" he asked.

"What's that?" I said.

He said these were from him, and he went out of the room, and he came right back in with a full bouquet of my favorite flowers.

It had lilies, roses, and some carnations, and a little foliage. They were beautiful and they screamed, "I LOVE YOU." It was huge and had a teddy bear.

"Awe." I said. "You didn't need to do that! Can I have the bear now in my bed?" I asked.

"Of course you can," he said smiling.

"You have been by my side, and you literally saved me." I said.

"I know," he said, "and don't you forget it. I love you, Mac. More now than ever." He said, "It really hit me when we almost lost you. I couldn't imagine my life without you. You are so strong and such a fighter. You've been through hell, and now here you are, you fought your way back to us, Mac." Levi continued.

"I've been sitting next to you planning our next date, and the date after that, and after that. I wouldn't even let the thought of losing you get in my head. So basically, we have a lot of dates to go on when you feel better."

"LOTS", I smiled big.

It just hit me, "Oh no, I must look like a hot mess," I said.

Levi said I never looked more beautiful, and seeing my beautiful green eyes again made me look even more beautiful! I told Levi that I wanted to take a shower so bad, but according to the doctors, it might be a little while. I was attacked when I got home from working at Sonic, so I was already nasty and needed a shower. But the nurse said my bandages are required to stay dry, and I was too weak to try a shower. They had been giving me sponge baths and would continue to do so. I wanted to ask the nurse at least for a toothbrush and toothpaste and a hairbrush.

Then, Levi saw Mandi out my room's window and said, "Coming right up," and he was out the door.

Just as he left, Mandi came in. She had tears in her eyes and hugged me and held my hand. "You scared us, Mac, you really did!" she said, crying. "I never thought I'd get to talk to you again, except in this bed or a gravestone."

"I'm a fighter," I said jokingly, but not.

I was a fighter. I think I proved that I'd die before I gave up to this coward. I thanked her for the flowers she sent me. I told her Levi read all the messages to me. Then I told her that I knew who he was.

"Who?" she asked.

I said, "remember at the bar, the guy that drugged me and tried to take me home at the club like forever ago?".

"No way," she said.

"Yup, it was him. I don't know why, but it was him."

She was glad that I recognized him. I told her I shot him but didn't kill him, and he was still out there. She said she heard the whole story except what happened before Levi came in, nobody knew except me and I was in a coma. So, I filled her in, and she said she couldn't imagine going through what I did. She said she couldn't be that strong. I told her she would, she's a strong person too, and almost as stubborn as me. She laughed.

"Shooting him, having two stab wounds and all, and while I was about to lose consciousness, I think I did well, hitting him," I said.

She laughed, and I tried not to. It still hurts too much.

"I can't wait to get out of here." I told her.

"Hopefully, it will be soon, but Mac, you suffered multiple serious injuries. You need to take it slow," she said. She knows me so well.

Then she said, "I know he was about to rape you."

I added, "and abduct me afterward."

She said, "You need to get mental help too. You need to take care of your mind. You've been going through hell for a while now. Please consider getting professional help, Mac." she finished.

"I will. I need it, I know I do." I said.

It's just not a priority right now, I thought. *My physical health is.*

I asked her if she had heard that the dagger he used on me was the same dagger he used on both Levi and Jaden. She said, "I heard that, and that the DNA from both of them was still on the dagger, under the handle. And now your DNA too." she continued, "and now It was in the police evidence locker."

My parents returned, so Mandi left. I told her I loved her, and she said she loved me too. I thanked her again for the flowers and told her they were beautiful! I thanked her for hanging out with me while I was still in a coma. She said I was welcome, and she'd be back after class. She gave both of my parents a hug, and off she went.

My parents came back into my room. They told me the doctor was ordering a hospital-type bed for me to help me get in and out without causing further damage to my wounds. The dagger had gone straight through my abdomen and also my chest, so I kind of had four wounds. I'd also need a shower chair and a nurse to stay with me when they were at work but they both had decided they were taking a month off to take care of me.

"A MONTH?" I asked loudly.

"It's going to take that long, are you kidding?" I said.

"Makayla, we are not kidding. You are hurt worse than you know. Probably because you just woke up. Soon, you will have to start sitting up, getting to the bathroom when they remove your catheter, and brushing your hair, so much Makayla."

I started to cry again but stopped because it hurt so bad.

"You were attacked only eight days ago. Remember how long it took Levi to get back to himself? He wasn't injured nearly as bad as you were." My dad said.

"OK," I said.

That was all I could muster out. Then I looked out the window and I saw Levi. We met eyes and he waved at me. My mom turned around and then smiled at me. She said she and my dad would take care of getting what I needed to come home, and I could visit with Levi some more.

Levi was all smiles, he went to the local store and got me a toothbrush and toothpaste, a brush, deodorant, some body spray, some M&Ms, and a few other things. "Wow," I said, "You thought of it all!"

He said he knew how much I hated feeling yucky, and hoped all this helped, then he gave me a kiss. I went ahead and used some of the body spray, it smelled amazing.

"Now to wash my greasy hair," I said. "I wasn't sure when the nurse was going to be able to do that."

Levi said, "Look in the bag."

I opened the bag and looked inside. He bought me dry shampoo, SCORE!

"Thank you so much, Levi!" I said.

Then Levi opened everything up and threw away the wrappers and cardboard backings. He kept my room nice and tidy. He knows how much messes bother my OCD. He knows me so well. He knows me like someone knows someone when they are head over heels in love. I smiled just thinking that.

The nurse came in and said, "You have another delivery, Makayla," and handed me another bouquet of flowers.

"Thank you," I said.

The flowers were so heavy because of my wounds. I asked Levi to take it and hand me the card, and he put them with the other flowers. I opened the card, and I froze. The card said, "I hope you heal up quickly. I still have plans for you, you have no idea how much fun we are going to have."

I couldn't move, I couldn't talk. Levi took the note and read it.

"Son of a Bitch," he yelled.

"Please throw those flowers out in the hallway, Levi." I asked.

"With pleasure," he replied.

"Keep the note for Officer John to add to evidence, please."

The visions from the evening he attacked me, started racing through my mind. The sound of his zipper. Being zip tied. Him touching my breasts. Being stabbed, smacked, kicked, and dragged by my hair, almost raped, all of it.

Chapter 12: Recovery

Four months later, I was fully recovered. It was a lot of work. Far more than I expected, and it was hard. I left my last physical therapy appointment, and I got some funny skeleton t-shirt with "I Love Physical Therapy" written on the back. I've been going there for two months. I started going there after two months of physical therapy at home. I texted Levi and told him that I was finished with physical therapy, and I have officially recovered!

But not quite mentally recovered, yet, I thought to myself.

But I was working on it. I had to continue therapy for a while. Years they said. Every time I heard a zipper I had flashbacks. I was kind of shocked I could wear my uniform for Sonic since that's what I was wearing when my stalker cut my shirt open and pulled down my pants.

Two months after the attack, I started working at Sonic again. My parents didn't want me to, but I had to do something. I was getting so bored sitting around the house and was only working part-time. I was also planning on going back to school next semester. I hadn't heard anything from my stalker since the flowers in the hospital. Not a peep. I hope that meant it was over.

My phone dinged. I got a text back from Levi, he texted me "Great, I'm so glad you are recovered! I have some plans for us!" I was intrigued.

"What's plans?" I texted back.

Then my phone rang, it was Levi. "Hello, my love." I said.

"Right back at you," he said.

I asked him again what was going on and he said it was a surprise.

"Can you tell me the dress code at least?" I asked.

He said, "Anything comfortable."

I went home and got a quick shower. I saw the scars on my abdomen and chest in the mirror as I undressed. Images from that night started flashing through my mind. I had to stop and focus on my new lease on life and my incredible boyfriend.

Levi said he'd pick me up after work around four o'clock. I was excited. I was ready to get on with my life, post stalker. I smiled. I was sure that he was done with me, and I was finally free of him and being scared, all the protection, and so on. However, I did decide I was going to buy another gun, just in case. I contacted my 'dealer' as you could say, and we met behind Panera after I got dressed. It was a quick transaction because I knew exactly what I wanted, so no dark alleys this time. I decided not to name my gun this time, laughing to myself.

Four o'clock came around and Levi was at the door. "Are you ready," he asked.

"I think so," I said.

"I would really like to know where we are going," I said.

He said it was about 20 minutes away. I looked out the window of his car, just watching the trees fly by. I had so much on my mind, but I didn't want that to ruin my date with Levi. Then I looked at Levi as he was driving. He looked amazing. I decided to put some music on. We both liked the same music, so it was easy. We both started singing along to the music.

I was so lucky to have survived my stalker, and so was Levi. I guess we are like a power couple now. Soon we pulled into the axe-throwing establishment. I was so excited!! I loved our axe-throwing date, our first date!

"Levi," I said, "you are too sweet! Back to where our first date was."

"I thought that might make you smile," he said.

We went in and got a table and a cage to throw the axes. I didn't do as good as I did on our first date, but I was still hitting the target. We did about three rounds and I was throwing hard. Every flashback of his face, hearing his zipper, the pain from the stabbing, cutting off my clothes, the look in his eyes as I crawled away, the eerie way he was staring at me just watching me die, everything flooded my mind, and I took it out on the target. Levi could tell. I just couldn't do it anymore. I was wiped.

I apologized to Levi, and he said, "Mac, it's absolutely no problem. I thought that you might be done after round two. You are such a fighter. One of the many reasons why I love you so much."

I smiled and laid a big kiss on him. I parted my lips, and we embraced and had a nice long kiss. Totally PDA. I didn't care. Levi settled the tab and then drove me to Lions Lake!

Lions Lake was one of my favorite places. The sun was still up. He brought two loaves of bread so we could feed the ducks, another one of my favorite things to do. It was so peaceful there and the ducks and one goose knew me at this point. It had been a while, so they were a little skittish, with Levi there too, that didn't help. But once they saw the bread, they were all over it. We fed them out of our hands and threw pieces to the ones too scared to come up to us.

The sunset was beautiful. We sat there and just took it in.

"Levi," I said.

"Yea," he replied.

"Thank you for the best evening I've had in I don't know how long," I said.

He had a huge smile on his face and said he'd do anything to put a smile on my face. And he sure did. We sat on the bench still watching the sun set, then he held my hand and put his other hand lightly on my face and turned my face toward him. We just stared into each other's eyes, and slowly moved toward each other and embraced for a kiss. A nice long, sweet kiss. It wasn't like making out. It was like true love exploding from our bodies. Each kiss was screaming, "I love you." He was the one, for sure. I think he felt the same way. I was 18 and he was 19 so I knew we weren't getting married right away, but I knew that we would eventually.

It was summer so the sun didn't fully set until about 8:30p.m. The colors were beautiful. I love watching sunsets.

Levi asked, "should we go?"

I answered, "Yea, let's get out of here." I was getting really tired.

He said "OK, I'll take you home, Mac."

When we pulled up to my house, Levi got out and walked me to the door. I asked him to come in. He did for a little while. No one was home. I armed the security system, and we settled in on the couch. He brushed the hair out of my face and kissed me. I loved kissing Levi. We made out off and on as we talked about several things, mostly about each other. I learned even more about Levi. I had no idea he volunteered at the boys and girls club, that was so awesome. He taught them jiujitsu and was a role model and Godly mentor to these kids that didn't have a good role model. That made Levi even more perfect in my eyes.

I told him how I volunteered at the church by serving food at events and then in the admin department, doing data entry. Then I would help out at the animal shelter when I had time. Before I didn't have time to do any of that, but since the attack, I had a lot more time. It was also part of my recovery mentally. He knew about the animal shelter but not the church volunteering.

He had been there for about an hour, and he could see how wiped I was so he gave me a quick kiss and said he was going to leave so I could get some rest. I walked him to the door and turned off the alarm. He told me not to forget to turn it on when he left. I assured I wouldn't. It was a habit at this point. I never forgot. I watched him walk to his car through the window, then went to my room to get my comfy clothes on and started getting ready for bed.

My room was upstairs now, in a actual bedroom. My parents decided to make the basement a rec room. They realized I had a lot of friends and thought it would be nice. They had a dart board, a pool table, shuffleboard, and a mini 'non-alcohol' bar. It looked awesome and was fun. My dad and I played pool a lot. All my friends were fan of the new rec room.

Shortly after getting all my makeup off and brushing my teeth, my parents got home. They asked me about my day. I told them that I was done with physical therapy, and Levi took me on a date. The first real date we've had since the attack. I told them about the axe-throwing, the sunset, Lions Lake and feeding the ducks, and that he came back here to talk for a bit. I said that it was the best evening I'd had in a long time.

They were really happy about my progress. They said they were putting my normal full-size bed back into my room this weekend. The medical device company was coming to get all the stuff we had to rent for my recovery.

Praise God, A real bed! I thought. My room would look like an actual room again and not a hospital room.

I asked them if they thought it was over, if my stalker was gone for good? They said they had no idea, but we should check in with Officer John and get his thoughts. But we needed to keep up the security protocols to be safe.

I was ready to start school again, and I knew that was potentially more dangerous. But then again, maybe he just decided I wasn't worth the trouble.

The next day I went to see Officer John. He said they knew who my stalker was. They were able to get prints off the dagger and DNA from my fingernails, and I was able to pick him out in pictures they showed me.

"What?" I asked. It's been four months! "Why am I just now hearing about this!" I demanded.

Officer John apologized but said it wasn't his call. He just got the clearance to tell me that afternoon and he planned on coming over to tell me the next day. My stalker finally had a name, it was Gabe Kingston. But they couldn't find him. He disappeared. I reminded them that he told me that we were going to "have a little fun, then go for a little ride."

I asked if maybe he was hiding out someplace secluded, maybe where he was going to take me.

He said, "That is very likely, but unfortunately we have zero idea of where that place could be."

Gabe never told me where or gave any hints. So, I had no idea where he was going to take me, only that he was taking me on a 'little' ride. Thank God Levi came when he did.

He showed me some items and asked if they were mine. They were in evidence bags. And yes! My favorite bra was in there and the knickknacks I noticed were missing. They recovered them all. I asked if I could have them back, but they said they needed to keep them in evidence. After the trial I could have them back. "Good," I said. Some of those were from my dad when he was overseas and I wanted them back.

The hunt was on for Gabe. His picture was on the news nearly every evening as a person of interest. They said his name was Gabe Kingston, and there was a reward for any tips leading to his capture.

Capture? I thought.

Put a ransom on his head instead and whoever kills him gets a payout. Save the taxpayers some money on him living in jail. I personally don't think he would allow anyone to catch him. It would be suicide by cop. Or he'd take his own life. He was far too prideful to let himself be taken by the police.

They had a profiler on my case now. His name was Officer Derma. He was tall and had brown skin, he was an older man with white hair. He was assigned my case because this stalking was going way too long and the attacks that have been made. Not just to me, but that he killed one person, and attacked two more. Getting away each time. They were hoping that he would be able to figure out why this was happening and how the police might find him.

Officer Derma wanted to question me. I told him the whole story from the beginning and how much he escalated. He asked about my life in general, the people in it, my home life, places I frequented, my romantic life, my classes and campus life, and so on.

I asked him, "Am I being interrogated as my own stalker." I laughed.

He laughed too. "No," he said, "but everything you can tell me can help me profile your stalker and hopefully find out where he is."

I asked him what was going to happen to me. "Do you think he is going to try and come back for me?'

Officer Derma asked, "When he had you on the floor, after he had straddled you, before he was going to rape you, did he make constant eye contact?"

I really didn't want to go through that part again. I heard his zipper again and I started to shake. I couldn't stop. He asked me if I would like a mild sedative to calm me down. I said, "Yes."

While we were waiting for that to kick in, he asked me about my different boyfriends during the time I was being stalked. I told him I had just broken up with Tommy. He was a total psycho, but he was already ruled out by the police.

I was involved with a guy from college named Jaden, but Gabe killed him. Then I met Levi when I signed up for jiujitsu, and we hit it off and are still dating. He was stabbed by Gabe as well.

"Oh," I remembered. "Things were missing from my room after one of the break ins, when he trashed my room. My favorite push up leopard designed bra. Also, some trinkets that my dad got me from various deployments."

I told him again that he cut off all my hair when I was asleep. "My hair was nearly to my low back, and he cut it so short, and well, you can see now how short it is, and it's grown out," Officer Derma was writing a lot down.

"Are you ready to talk about the near rape, Mac?" He asked

"No, but I'll try." I said.

"So," he repeated, "When he had you straddled and then between your legs, did he keep eye contact?"

"Yes," I said. "He told me not to close my eyes."

"When he said he needed you awake for this, was he still making eye contact?" He asked.

"Yes," I answered. "Why are you asking? What does it mean?"

He said, "Nothing just yet." He needed more details. "When he said you were going to have a little fun before you went on a little ride with him, was he still making contact?"

"Yes," I answered.

"When he stabbed you, the second time, did he keep eye contact?" He asked.

"Yes," I answered again, "Gabe even smiled. He was enjoying seeing me suffer and try to get away." I added.

What was up with all this eye contact stuff? I asked myself.

"Last question," he said. "When he smacked you, did he make eye contact?"

"I don't know," I answered. "I didn't look at him."

"Did he make you look at him after he smacked you?" He asked, again.

"Actually, yes." I answered. I said, "He grabbed my chin to force me to look at him," I continued.

"How many times did he do that, Mac?" He asked

I told him several times during the duration of the attack. "He even said he wanted me awake when he raped me," I said. "He told me, "I'm going to need you awake for this, Mac." I continued. "His words still haunt me, he was so eerie."

I told him that he injected me with something then I was wide awake. "He wanted me to be looking at him for everything he was doing. He was obsessed about it. But didn't care if he hurt me," I told the profiler.

Officer Derma jumped in. "Yes," he said. "Because he is obsessed with you, but his anger is out of control. He can't control it. And to him it's love. He expected you to behave but you did not."

Everything was starting to make sense. He said, "He most likely grew up in an abusive environment, most likely abused himself. He took that to mean love," he added.

I asked Officer Derma if he would ever stop. If this is over or is he still waiting for the perfect time to attack me again. Officer

Derma said it was not over. He will come back because he hasn't finished.

"He's proved how patient he can be. Waiting for the perfect moment. Based on all the information I have, again, he is obsessed with you, and he thinks he is in love with you, and you are in love with him… in his mind."

I asked him, "How can that be just by me talking to him at a bar for less than five minutes, and I wasn't even flirting?" Officer Derma said these things trigger stalkers because their reality is altered. The main reason they pick someone is because they felt "heard". And they want to be heard.

"Well, I am NOT giving him what he wants." I said, "I will do the exact opposite of everything he tells me to do."

Next, I asked him, "What can I do to stay safe? I've already done most of what was recommended."

"One other thing to add is that I would recommend you get a dog," he said. "A dog will alert you, and also most dogs will protect their owners."

"Wouldn't he just stab my dog, and continue on?"

"He might," he answered. "But dogs can be a deterrent too, and should sleep in your room. If the alarm doesn't get triggered, the dog will be barking and give you a chance to wake up and grab your pepper spray."

I didn't tell him I had a gun, but it would give me a chance to grab my gun as well.

"Did that give you any insight to where he might be, Officer Derma?"

"Yes," he said.

"I believe you are not his first stalking victim, and he most likely has a cabin or home in the woods nearby." He answered.

"He said a 'little' ride, so I would assume it's in this county and there are not a lot of woods here. I want to send officers out to all the forest areas and open farming areas to knock on doors of cabins or homes. He is held up somewhere that is away from roads, other homes, and he was going to take you there because no one would see or hear anything. But you spoiled his plans." He concluded.

"Can I be the bait, and can we draw him out?" I asked. He told me that was far too dangerous and could escalate him even more. "Even more? I don't think there is much more he can do to me," I said.

"You'd be surprised, Mac," he responded.

I was getting so frustrated. I wanted to move on with my life and it was time to get brave.

"What if he dropped me and is stalking another girl," I asked.

"He might have another girl in mind, but he won't stalk her and stop stalking you and abandon all his work. We have his picture on the evening news, not as a person of interest anymore, but as armed and dangerous criminal. He's coming back for you Makayla," he answered. "I'm 99.9% sure of it. And after what happened, stalking you isn't fun for him anymore. He is coming to tie loose ends and move on to his next victim, probably in another state since his picture is all over the news."

Chapter 13: The Story Unfolds

When Levi got to my street, I could see lights, news vans, and reporters. "What the hell?" I said. Levi shook his head and told me not to worry. We were going to plow past them and go straight into the house. I had my house key ready. He parked on the street, and I pulled my hoodie over my head, Levi had his arms around me and was blocking my face from the cameras.

I could see flashes coming from all around me. I could see the flashes of light through my hoodie.

Reporters were asking questions, and I couldn't make any of them out because they were all screaming them at me at once. "Almost there," Levi said. I could barely make out what he said. Several of the news stations were live. They were facing my home with a reporter standing in front of my house announcing that they were filming live. So many questions I couldn't make out.

I was able to make out one question, "What's it like being stalked?" That pissed me off. I turned around and looked at him, I pulled back the hood on my hoodie and started speaking.

"Everyone stop!" I yelled. "Please leave. I have been through hell and back and I need to rest. Do you not have any common decency to leave me alone? Get off my lawn and off my property or I will call the police. I'm not answering any questions. Now GO!" I told them.

Levi was holding the door open, he already disarmed the alarm. It was dead quiet for a few moments. Then the noise grew again, a knock on the door here and there, just so much commotion. Levi told me I didn't have to talk to them. I told him "I wasn't planning on it, but that reporter seriously pissed me off. Ugh, I should have just ignored him."

"It's OK, Mac," Levi said. "Let's just watch the news." I said OK, and we turned on the news to see live news in front of my house, then what I said was being replayed. Then a reporter started sharing my story. Almost all of it! I couldn't believe it. How the hell did they get that information? I couldn't do anything, but watch this reporter spill my traumatic life.

Levi asked if I was OK, I told him I was, but I wasn't. Levi knew I wasn't OK. It was written all over my face.

"Mac, we can talk about it if you want. I know you are not OK; how could you be?"

I started to tear up. "The whole area is going to know about what has been happening, they are sharing nearly all of it? They know about attempted rape, obviously the stabbing too, me shooting him, just about everything that happened that dreadful day and some events leading up to it. What about all the other crazy stuff? How much does the press know? This is my private life!" I exclaimed.

I continued my rant, "Levi, every time I hear a zipper it takes me back to being zip tied and about to be raped. I keep hearing him unzip his jeans," I continued. "Then I hear him in my head saying that he was going to show me what it's like being with a 'real man'." I said. I saw Levi make a fist when I said that.

"That's when I knew he was going to rape me. But he didn't, because of you, so why am I still having flashbacks?" Levi said, "You are suffering from PTSD, you know that. Your therapist will keep working on you with that."

"You are going to get past this, I know how strong you are, Mac, you have been through hell and back with this guy."

"So have you," I responded.

"Nothing compares to what you endured, Mac, and for how long. I've seen my share of thriller movies, and they don't hold a candle to what you are going through," he said. I asked him if it was too much for him. And if he wanted out, I understood. "I feel like damaged goods, just a shell of my old self," I said. "Mac, you are crazy if you think I would break it off with you." I smiled at him and gave him a kiss. "Thank you," I responded.

He said he would stay the night on the couch if it was alright with my parents, and I told him that would be fine. Then he wouldn't have to deal with the circus outside. My parents were out of state, anyway, visiting my great aunt who was dying. I was not cleared for travel yet by my doctor, so I couldn't go. I told them I'd be fine, and they should go. But since they were out of town, I told Levi he could sleep in my bed. I wanted nothing more than to fall asleep in his arms. I got ready for bed and got my pajamas on, washed my face and brushed my teeth. I took my medications and brushed my hair.

Levi's toothbrush was there in the bathroom, so he brushed his teeth. When I walked into my room, I saw him standing there, in his boxers, exposing his abs and his muscular thighs. He was so lean, and muscular, but not too much, just perfect.

Even with the night's events, I couldn't wait to fall asleep. We kept eye contact, which was hard because that's what Gabe kept making me do. He ruined that for me. But I found looking in Levi's eyes was different, and I loved staring in his eyes.

I put on my favorite playlist, and we started kissing as the music played. The look he gave me was so intense. I wanted to make love to him, and I know he was thinking the same. I could see it in his eyes, and I'm sure he could see it in mine.

Then I looked away. "Mac, what's wrong babe?"

"I told him that I hope he isn't disappointed I was saving myself for marriage," I said.

"No way babe, I'm not a virgin, but I don't sleep around. If you are waiting for marriage I totally respect that, and it gives us a reason to hurry up and get married. You are worth the wait." He said.

I was so relieved! And did he seriously just talk about marrying me?! "Well, in that case, I can breathe now because I really want to, and now." He said he did too, but we couldn't. I agreed.

We held each other and talked about just about everything, kissing here and there. He told me more about his family, and I talked about mine too. I told him how sweet his parents were when he was in the ICU. They told me they really liked me.

Suddenly there was a loud pounding on the door. Someone was yelling. Levi put on his jeans, and I put on a robe, and Levi went to the door. He told me to step back. It was a reporter. "Oh my gosh." I said, "are they ever going to leave?"

But then I heard him, he was yelling, "Have you heard? It's all over the news." Levi disarmed the house and cracked open the door. "Gabe was just found dead. He was shot in the forehead!" I couldn't believe it.

Levi shut the door and locked it and turned on the alarm, then he turned on the news. I sat there in my pajamas and robe and Levi in just his jeans. He was looking really sexy, but I couldn't think about that now.

There it was, the reporter talked about my stalking and then showed Gabe's picture and said he was found dead in his car on the south side of town. There were no leads as of now as to who killed him. Suicide had been ruled out. The reporters were leaving my front lawn and hurrying over to where Gabe was found dead.

I heard my phone ding; I had a text. Officer John said he was on his way over. "Awesome," I said loudly. "What's that, Mac?" Levi asked. "Officer John is on his way over. I bet we are going to get the full scoop of what happened!" I answered.

About 20 minutes later, Officer John knocked on the door. "Hi, Officer John," I said. The circus finally left just in time for you. They are all over the Gabe case now.

He greeted us and told us that Gabe was found about a mile from the house, in his car with one shot to his forehead. He said he had to question me because I was the prime suspect.

"WHAT?" I responded. He had to be kidding.

Officer John apologized, but he said he needed to question not just me, but Levi, my parents, my friends, and everyone who was close to this case. I understood but was really taken back by it. "Well, I hope you understand that I'm not sad in the least, and when you find out who did it, I'm going to throw them a party," I said. Officer John laughed.

I told him, "With the upmost respect to you, I apologize but neither Levi, nor I, will be answering any questions without an attorney present." Officer John said that it was well within our rights, and that we needed to come to the station tomorrow morning or afternoon with our lawyers and answer some questions.

"Thank you for not making us do this now," I said. "No problem, I understand. It's late and I mainly wanted to just check on you and see how you were holding up." He said.

"I really don't want to do this, Mac, I hope you can understand," he said. I told him I understood and that we'd see him tomorrow with our lawyers. I walked Officer John out and turned to Levi. I locked the door and turned on the alarm. "Can you believe this?" I asked Levi. "It's just protocol, Mac, I doubt anything will come of it. I suppose all of us have a motive." He said.

"Can we just go back to bed?" I asked tiredly. "I just want to lay in your arms where I feel safe and put this evening behind me." I explained "Most definitely," he said smiling.

I woke up the following day and Levi wasn't next to me. Where did he go? Then I smelled something, food, breakfast! Awe. He's making me breakfast. I wonder if I should stay in bed or go out there. I decided to get dressed, brush my teeth, and put on a little make up, and I snuck up behind him and hugged him from behind. "Mac!" he said. "Good morning my love," he continued. Michelle came into the kitchen and said it smelled good. Levi replied, "There is plenty for you too if you would like some." She said sure.

As we ate breakfast I told Michelle about last night. She said, "I saw, you seriously gave that reporter a piece of your mind." "Yea,

I kind of snapped when he asked me that question." I told her the police were going to question all of us. She had no idea anyone killed my stalker, Gabe. She said, "Well I won't be shedding any tears, and they can ask me all the questions they want." I agreed, "Same here, sister" I continued. I called mom and dad, and they got us a lawyer. We are going after breakfast if you want to come with us and get it over with," I said. Michelle said she would.

"I just now realized…it's over! Yes, I have to deal with questioning, but in the end, it's over! I'm safe now!" I said cheerfully. I started to tear up, happy tears and disbelief. Levi got up from the table and hugged me from behind. I turned around and stood up and hugged him so tightly. "It's over, for real this time. I'm free." "Yes, you are," Levi agreed. "It's over," I repeated.

I had several news stations and also talk show hosts calling me for an interview from around the US. Quite frankly, I was shocked my little story was going national. I told them all I had to think about it. I asked what Levi thought. He said, "It's your story to tell or not tell." I decided to do it. But not to the news.

I decided to tell my story in an interview with Paul Freud. I've seen a few of his interviews, and he doesn't interrupt, there are no time limits, he uses the extra part of the interview for the next episode if we run over. Also, it's mandatory that the audience stay quiet. No questions, nothing. He was gentle, and If I couldn't talk about something, he wouldn't make me. Also, if I wasn't OK with a live audience, he would do it without one.

I called his personal assistant and formally agreed to tell my story. But I wanted the interview to focus on surviving and not giving up. I didn't want to make what Gabe did to me to be the bulk of my story. I didn't want to give him any glory. And I didn't want it to be a big victim story. I wanted people to hear what I've been through, but also be inspired to be brave and always have hope and know God's got them. I wanted to teach women to understand how to defend themselves, and other things like that. Maybe Levi could help with that. I also wanted several tickets for my family and one up close for Levi in case it starts getting too hard. They agreed to my terms, so my interview was scheduled for next week and I told them it was OK with a live audience.

I told Levi about the interview in next week, and told him they gave me a front row ticket so that way I could look at you if I started to have a hard time. He said, "I'll be there, I was already planning on trying to get a ticket."

I called my family over and I had my mom and dad on speaker. I told them that I was doing an interview with Paul Freud. "They are giving me five tickets, not including Levi's. So, who wants to go?" My mom said she didn't know if she was up to hearing all the details, but she felt the need to. She wanted to know every detail of what happened so she could support me. Michelle wanted a ticket, and so did Mandi if any were left over. I told her "Of course I have one for you, you are my bestie!" My dad said he'd claim one too.

"Awesome," I said. I have one left. I'll ask Kaye, then Misty if they want to come.

I was kind of excited, I told them. I could finally get my story out there, and only have to tell the story once. "All of Paul Freud's interviews get uploaded to YouTube. So, people who ask I can send them there or to Paul's website. Then, it's finally over! I get to go back to school, back to work, just live a normal life again, with the love of my life!" I exclaimed.

My mom chimed in, "Just don't be in a hurry to move out again." "Well mom, it's going to happen, but not right away," I smiled.

After breakfast, Levi and I were cleaning up the kitchen. I decided to flirt with him and grabbed a kitchen towel, rolled it up a little, and snapped it on Levi's butt. "OUCH" he called out. I couldn't stop laughing and said I was sorry. He laughed and grabbed the other kitchen towel and was about to do the same, so I ran, he caught up with me in the hallway and SNAP, he got me on the butt. I laughed so hard.

Then Levi pinned me against the wall and gave me a deep long kiss. I kissed him back and I heard Michelle say, "Get a room guys." "I think we will," I said jokingly. "Don't be jealous Michelle." I laughed. She rolled her eyes and said she'd meet us at the police station, with our lawyers. "OK," I said, "We'll meet you there. Probably be ready to leave in 15 minutes so go ahead and answer questions with our lawyer and tell her I'm right behind you." "OK," she said and was out the door.

I told Levi we could finish cleaning up after we went to the station. We needed to get ready. He said he was going to run home and take a shower and get a change of clothes and he'd meet me there. I told him OK, and I loved him, he said he loved me too and he was out the door. I took a quick shower myself and wore some nice jeans with a non-flashy yellow patterned blouse. I wore my favorite pair of tennis shoes. I did my hair and makeup and grabbed my keys and purse then I opened the front door while digging in my purse for my sunglasses. I bumped right into somebody standing on the porch. "Sorry," I said as I lifted my head to see who I hit.

Oh my gosh! *Tommy.*

"What are you doing here?" I asked him. "I need to leave, like now, Tommy." He didn't move. He just stared at me. "Good to see you again, Makayla," he finally spoke. Since when does he call me Makayla? I thought. "Well, I can't say the same, Tommy. Please leave or I'll call the police." I told him.

Then he pulled a syringe from his pocket. I looked at the syringe, and I dropped my purse and turned to run but he grabbed my arm and plunged the needle in my shoulder. I stumbled back and he started smiling.

"It should take full effect in a couple minutes." He said smugly. "I wish I knew how easy this could have been in the beginning. But Gabe just had to be the one to roofie you at the bar. He was an idiot." He said.

My eyes were getting heavy, I stumbled around the house, trying to get away and I knocked a few things over, and then I collapsed. The curtains started to close. The last thing I saw was Tommy standing over me.

It's not over.

Chapter 14: Levi

I got to the police station, and they had just finished up with Michelle. "How was it?" I asked Michelle. "Not bad," she replied. Officer John saw me and asked me where Mac was. "She's right behind me. She should be here anytime." I turned to Mac's lawyer, Kendra Brentwood, and asked, "can you hang out here until she gets here?" I asked. "Of course I can. I'm getting paid by the hour," she replied with a smile. Mac's parents obviously weren't needing to be questioned because they had an alibi, they've been out of the state.

Officer John questioned me with my lawyer. It took about 30 minutes to finish. He asked where I was between 12 p.m. and 4 p.m. yesterday. I told him, "I was with Mac, and we were just cruising around in my Jeep." I continued, "When Mac is having a rough day, she loves cruising in my Jeep with the top off and doors off. Then I took her to speak with the profiler. After that, we stopped and grabbed something to eat at Wiggly, the barbeque place. After that, we cruised around some more." I said.

Officer John asked what we did after that. I said, "Well that night I brought her home and the news stations were all over her front lawn. We didn't know someone leaked her story."

Officer John apologized again about that. He said they found out that one of the officers was paid for the scoop, and he took the bribe and told them everything he knew. He has been fired and we are charging him as well. Mac will have her day in court with him." My lawyer chimed in, "and tell Mac that she can sue the police station and the city as well."

Then officer John asked for my fingerprints, but my lawyer spoke up and said that was not standard protocol. Officer John said it was to rule out his fingerprints at the crime scenes. My lawyer wasn't having it, so Officer John backed down. "I'll give you my fingerprints," I said. They quickly brought in ink and the fingerprint kit. He asked me if I hated Gabe enough to kill him. I said, "If my main objective was to kill him, I would have finished him off after Mac shot him." Officer John wrote down his answer. He asked several more questions and let me go. Officer John thanked me for coming in and I said it was no problem, and my lawyer left.

I wanted to stay and wait for Mac. *Where is Mac?* I thought. A few minutes later I got a phone call from Michelle. Before I could even say hello, Michelle said "Is Mac with you?" clearly panicked. "No, why, what's wrong?" I asked. "I just got home, and the front door was wide open. I figured Mac just didn't shut it all the way, but then I found a syringe on the floor by the front door, and her purse spilled over. There are some things that have been knocked down and on the ground."

I yelled for Officer John. I told him everything Michelle told me. Officer John told me to tell Michelle not to touch anything and that he and several officers would make their way there. Forensics were on the way as well. Michelle texted me and told me she thinks Mac has been abducted. Her car was still there, and there was clearly a struggle. I texted her back not to worry, wait on the police, they were on the way.

All I could do was pray that she was alright. This made no sense. The stalker was dead, who would have possibly abducted her? I love her so much. I can't bear the thought that she might be with some psycho. Maybe her story on the news got her a new stalker? What if she's hurt?

Mac, babe, I love you. Where are you? That was all I could think of on my way to her house. I figured Michelle might need a friendly face until their parents arrived. Oh yea, her parents. Someone needs to tell them.

I called Michelle, "Michelle, can you call your parents and let them know what is going on?" he asked. She said she already had. They didn't answer so she left a voicemail. They were probably still in the air and hadn't landed yet. "They are going to be so upset," she told me. "I know," I said.

When I got to Mac's house there were police everywhere, Michelle was on the front lawn talking to an officer that was taking notes. I guess this is a crime scene now. I wondered if they were going to let me stay. Officer John was there so my chances were good.

I got out of my Jeep and walked towards Michelle. Officer John came over and stopped me. "You need to leave, Levi," he told me. He explained that this was a crime scene, and he didn't need more people there that could potentially ruin the evidence. "I'm here for Michelle, her parents aren't back yet, and she is really upset," I told him. Officer John rubbed his chin and said, "Fine, just stay out of the way and stay outside if you can until forensics has finished." "Will do," I said.

I continued walking towards Michelle just as the officer that was questioning her started walking off. She saw me and gave me a hug. She had obviously been crying. Her mascara was running, and she had 'racoon' eyes. "I'm so glad you are here, Levi," she said. "Of course," I told her. Then I asked her what she told that cop and what all he was asking. She said they believe she was abducted. They were taking the syringe to the lab to see if one, her DNA was on the needle, and two, what was in it. "It's OK, Michelle," I started saying, "Mac is tough, you know this, she's going to get herself freed and come back to us, or the police will find her. Either way we will get her back safe." Michelle cried some more.

I remembered what Mac told me about types of stalkers. Their main goal is to get their victims to acknowledge them. So, she had to know her abductor, or maybe, like I thought earlier, some sicko that saw the news coverage decided he'd pick up where Mac's stalker left off. I decided to share my theory with Officer John. I got his attention, and he came out to the front lawn where Michelle and I were.

I asked if he had anything to go on. "Well, she was obviously abducted. None of the neighbors saw anything though. So, we don't have much to go on unless forensics finds something. They are working on it now. They just left so you can go inside." He said. He started walking off and I asked him to wait a minute. "I have a theory. What if some sicko saw the news coverage and decided to pick up where Mac's stalker left off?" I asked. Officer John said that was a good theory. He would keep that in mind. He said again that they are working with basically nothing. He said they had some other theories to go on, but he couldn't discuss that with us.

Michelle was shaking so I held her tight and told her to breathe. Where are you, Mac? I thought to myself. I walked Michelle inside and Mandi pulled up. She walked right in and asked what happened. "I was coming to celebrate with Mac and that she was finally free and out of danger. What's up with all the cops, and forensics? Is she dead?" Mandi asked frantically.

"No! she's not dead, but she's been abducted. She was supposed to be answering questions at the police department but never showed. Michelle called me and she said the door was wide open and there was a syringe on the floor and her purse, and stuff knocked over. Definitely a struggle." I finished. Mandi was at a loss. We all were. I got Michelle and Mandi to sit in the living room until we got word of what happened.

I walked by the kitchen and saw the dirty dishes from breakfast that we were both cleaning up. I reminisced about us flirting and snapping kitchen towels at each other.

Mac, baby, please be ok, I pleaded.

An hour went by, and we didn't hear anything from Officer John. We still couldn't reach Mac's parents, but they were due to land in about an hour. And it's an hour drive from the airport. I wanted them to know as soon as possible.

I had to stay busy, so I finished cleaning up the kitchen. Then I went around and picked up some of the trash the forensics team left. Wrappers and things like that. I checked on Michelle and Mandi, and they were both holding up the best they could. They asked if I had heard anything, but I hadn't. Their faces looked so bleak. I'm sure mine did too.

I went and stood in front of both of them. I asked, "Is Mac tough?" "Yes they replied, perplexed, I continued. "Is Mac a quitter?" They both said no. "Is Mac a fighter?" They both said yes. "Can Mac handle herself?" Yes they said again. "Does Mac get what she wants?" "Yes," they answered again, wondering what Levi was doing. "Is Mac stubborn?" another yes with some excitement now. They were both perking up. "Then I would say we have a very good chance of getting her back. She knows a ton of self-defense strategies, she's tough, stubborn, she never quits or backs down from anything and she knows how to manipulate and mess with people's minds. Whoever has her has no idea what they are in for, right?" I finished. They agreed. I think I needed that pep talk as much as they did, as corny as it was.

Michelle said, "the cops have nothing to go on." "Not yet," I responded. "There is always something. Maybe there is something the cops missed, that we might find because we know her. Mac WILL find a way to save herself, or give the cops something to go on." I started looking around the front door where she was abducted to see if I could find anything the cops may not have seen as a clue. Moments later, Michelle and Mandi were doing the same. I looked in her purse, then on the carpet in the entryway, then looked around the items that were knocked over in the struggle, even on the walls.

Wait a minute. I looked closer. I see a letter T scratched into the paint. Just barely. If the light hadn't shone just as it was right now, I would have never seen it. I yelled for Michelle. "Have you seen this T before?" "No," she answered. "Do you think it means anything, or just a scratch no one has noticed?" she asked. "I don't know," I said, but I'm taking a picture of it and texting it to Officer John." Michelle said, "It almost looks like it could be a J." Mandi agreed. And it did. So was Mac making a T and just whatever she was injected with made it look like a J from sliding down the wall, or was it a J. Or was it nothing at all. I took pictures from several angles. Officer John texted back, "thank you, but don't touch it. I'm coming back with just one forensics officer to look at it."

She may have been trying to give us an initial before the injection kicked in. Officer John and another officer took pictures and dusted for prints. They paid real close attention to the letter on the wall, and the forensics officer unpackaged a sealed cotton swab to see if there was DNA inside the scrape. If not, it might have always been there, and it got scratched by furniture, or a wall hanging. The possibilities were endless.

"Please let us know as soon as you find out anything, Officer John," I requested. He said he would, and to keep my phone handy. We were all in better spirits. Just waiting, it's the worst. So, we shared memories of Mac. I heard a lot of stories I'd never heard before. Then my phone rang. It was Officer John.

"Yes, Officer John, what did you find out?" "Well, Makayla did make that scratch in the wall, her DNA from her fingernails was found inside the scratch and in multiple places throughout the letter. Does the letter T or J mean anything to any of you?" He asked. "Just a minute," I said. "Michelle, Mandi, does the letter T or J mean anything to you guys?" There was a long pause and they both said no.

I started to tell Officer John goodbye, and Michelle said, "WAIT!"

"What's up Michelle," I said. "She dated a guy named Tommy, and she dated a guy named Jaden. I doubt it means anything, especially since we don't know what the letter actually is, a J or a T," she continued. "But Jaden is dead, Tommy, the psycho turned crybaby, is still alive. But he's not your guy. He's too much of a baby. Plus, they already ruled him out of the stalking." Michelle finished.

I told Officer John everything that Michelle had said and we hung up. "That's awesome Michelle. Hopefully that will help." Then I had a sickening thought. What if it's the cop that helped her all along. Maybe the J was for Officer John. I've watched movies with that kind of twist. I didn't want to share my theory with the girls, but I was going to keep an extra eye on Officer John. How he acts, talks, and reacts. What if during this case he became obsessed with her. But, he was taking my fingerprints when she was abducted. So, I guess it couldn't be him. But I was going to pay more attention just in case. Come on Mac, give us something! I begged.

Officer John was on his way over to be there when Mac's parents arrived and filled us all in on what was going on. We all stayed at Mac's parents' house until he got there.

Chapter 15: Abducted

When I opened my eyes, I was zip tied and in the trunk of Tommy's car. We were still in the city, I heard a church bell ring. Thank God I thought. I untied my shoelaces like Levi taught me and tied them to each other. I took the zip tie and kicked my feet back and forth as fast as I could to create the heat to break through the zip tie, then finally, they snapped. My hands were free. I kicked off my shoes. I didn't have time to untie them and re-tie them, especially with a giant knot.

OK, feel around Mac, there has to be an emergency pull cord in here. Yes! I said as I felt around it. I praised God in my head. I waited for the car to stop. It took forever, he must be hitting all green lights. *Please don't get on the highway yet, please!* I prayed. Then the car finally stopped. I pulled the cord, and the trunk opened right up, and I crawled out and started waving down cars while I ran from Tommy's trunk.

Some people got out of their cars. *I'm saved*, I thought. Then I suddenly felt his arms grab my waist. Tommy got out of the car and chased me down. More people were getting out of their cars to help me, but then Tommy pulled out his gun and shot once into the air. So, everyone backed up.

I saw a lot of people on their phones, probably calling the police. Some were just taking videos. Hopefully that will help the cops. Tommy dragged me to the trunk literally kicking and screaming and shoved me in. I didn't make it easy for him. Then he pulled out his pocket knife and cut the emergency cord, and then used his lighter to make it shrivel all the way back into its little hole.

Damn, I thought. I begged him to let me go but he just slammed the trunk closed. Then he peeled out and he was going fast.

He was swerving and I was being thrown around in his trunk, and I'm assuming he was also running red lights because I kept hearing honking. Then one last curve sent me to the other side of the trunk. We were going straight now on a smooth road. The dang highway, I thought. We were only on it for about five minutes, then a turn sent me rolling the other direction in the trunk. The trunk was pretty large. I started feeling around to see if there was a tire iron or something. Then we went to the side roads. I could tell because I felt all the bumps for a while now, so I knew we were heading far into the country. I couldn't find a weapon. How am I getting out of this one?

It's Tommy, the crybaby, I can get away from him. Or at least I hoped. Did he stalk me? Or did he just get his friend Gabe too. Were they friends? I was so confused, and I wanted answers. I figured maybe a way to soften him up is to ask him why he was doing this, and where did Gabe fit in, Did Tommy kill him? And who did what stalking. He had to be the one behind all this, so he had to have killed Gabe, but why? If none of the violent ones were done by him, then maybe I had a better chance of getting out of this situation. Gabe had no hesitation to hurt me. Will Tommy?

The car finally stopped, and I heard Tommy open and close his door. Then I heard him walk around to the trunk. The trunk opened and Tommy pulled me out and zip tied my hands again. I used the same trick I used with Gabe. I made it look like my hands were close together when they weren't. But Tommy zip tied each hand separately like handcuffs. Well, no getting out of these. Tommy kept his hands on my zip tie cuffs and walked me into this little farm home. The rocks hurt my bare feet. He shut the door, he injected me with some sedative again, I tried to fight him and get away, but the curtains closed again.

When I came to, my hands were zip tied to a drainpipe in the damp basement. It smelled of mildew and had very little light. *Where the hell am I?* I thought. My vision was blurry, and I felt like I was hungover. *What did he inject me with?* The zip ties were tight. There was no getting out of them. I was utterly helpless, and at the mercy of this psycho.

My wrists hurt so badly. I tried to pull the ties from the drain, but it wasn't working. "OK, Mac, how are we getting out of this one?" I said out loud to myself. I looked around to take in my surroundings, and to see if there was anything that could help me. There wasn't much of anything. I saw a cot to my far left, and there was a full bath that had studs up but no drywall yet. It looked like he was working on a downstairs guest suite because I saw more studs surrounding a large area. I saw the door, and *what was that?* I squinted my eyes, the door had a Ring doorbell device on it. *Oh my gosh, He's watching me!* How did I not know Tommy was literally crazy.

I tried tugging again at the zip ties. Nothing. Ugh. I looked around some more and there were a couple windows, but I couldn't escape from them. There were bars over the visible window, the rest were covered. I assumed they all had bars on them. The window was also high up there, and small. I could definitely get through it, but I would need a ladder, and no bars. Maybe I could get Tommy to open the other windows for more light.

"Tommy?" I yelled.

"I know you are watching me, come in here," I shouted.

"TOMMY, ANSWER ME," I screamed.

Why was he not answering me? A few moments later, I heard what sounded like a padlock click and then metal on metal...a latch maybe? He opened the door. And there stood Tommy. "Why did you abduct me?" I asked, "What do you want with me?" He didn't answer. He just kept staring at me. "Answer me," I yelled. Then he finally spoke.

"I want you to realize the mistake you made dumping me, out of nowhere," he said. *What?* I thought. "Isn't this a little extreme?" I asked. "You know how it goes; extreme times call for extreme measures." "What exactly are the extreme times here, Tommy" I asked. "Obviously I know the extreme measures." I said.

"All I ever wanted was a chance to talk to you, to make you realize you still loved me. But you shut the door in my face." he continued, "Do you have any idea how bad that hurt me?"

Seriously? All this is because I dumped him.

"I was talking with my bud, and he said he could arrange for us to be alone to talk. He said he'd drug your drink and bring you here. It was his idea. Then you would have to talk to me. He was supposed to bring you to me so we could talk it out. But he screwed that all up. Idiot."

Are you talking about Gabe?" I asked. "Yes," he said. "When that didn't work, I started following you just to see when I could catch you, alone, and we could go somewhere private and talk." he said.

Then when I had to work, Gabe would follow you for me and give me reports of where you were and who you were with." he said. "Here I was trying to find a way to fix things and then you, YOU, already got yourself a new boyfriend." He screamed.

"Are you talking about Jaden?" "YES" he yelled. "So naturally I was pissed," he said. "So, you had Gabe kill Jaden?" I asked. "Yes," he admitted. It was Gabe's idea," he said. "But you gave the OK?" I asked. "Yes," he said. "Then that makes you a killer, Tommy." I said.

"He said he promised if you were single again, it would help me get what I wanted, YOU," he said. "I knew if I could just talk to you, we would make things work." He stated.

"Jaden and I were broke up when you had him killed," I stated. "How was I supposed to know that?" he asked. "You moved on quickly and landed a new boyfriend, Levi." He said. "Did you have Gabe try to kill him too?" I asked. "Yes," he answered. And Gabe screwed that up. He showed his face too. "You bastard, how could you? I had no idea you were so evil." I shouted at him.

"I decided to scare you until you stayed home so I could talk to you. Because apparently my feelings weren't returned, I just wanted you to see me and hear me out!"

Then I asked, "So you made my life hell and stalked me with your buddy? You think that is love?" I asked.

"Yes", he replied.

"AND HAVING YOUR FRIEND STAB ME, NOT ONCE, BUT TWICE, NEARLY KILLING ME BY THE WAY, AND LETTING HIM RAPE ME, YOU CALL THAT LOVE TOO?" I screamed as loudly as I could at him.

"HELL NO!" he shouted back. "THAT'S WHY I KILLED THAT SON OF A BITCH" He shouted.

"One shot straight to his forehead," he bragged. "Hurting you was not part of our arrangement. And he was trying to take what was mine. Your virginity. I couldn't stand for that." he said. "I was going to kill him anyway, but I had no idea he did all of that to you until I saw the news," he promised.

"So, the news told you how he stabbed me and then forced me to turn off the alarm. Then he shot me up with something because I wouldn't hold still?" I continued. "Did the news tell you how, as he unzipped his pants, that I was going to see what it's like to be with a real man." I asked.

"Then, because I wouldn't hold still, he stabbed me again. He smacked me around, too. Did the news tell you all that? Did the news tell you that at the lake, he pretended to be Levi twice, once dancing behind me and rubbing me up and down, then in bed pulling down my shoulder straps and kissing my shoulders? Did the news tell you that?" He was silent

I could go on and on, Tommy. Shall I?

"You unleashed a monster on me, Tommy! How could you?"

"I'm so sorry, Makayla. Gabe swore to me it wasn't him."

"And you believed him? Seriously? Did you not see his sketch on the news? Did you wonder how he got shot?" I asked. "You were played, Tommy, the whole time he played you, he wanted me for himself. How does that feel?" I asked, rubbing it all in his face.

Then Tommy punched the concrete wall.

"I get it, I screwed up. I trusted someone I shouldn't have," Tommy said. "But that doesn't change why I did it. I did all of this because I love you." He said.

"Now who sounds obsessed?" I snapped back at him.

"Gabe was the one who pretended to be your brother. He called on speaker phone" Tommy said. "Who sent the disturbing note with flowers?" I asked. "I don't know what you are talking about, Makayla. That must have been Gabe." Tommy said.

"Did he think I wouldn't find out?" he asked out loud.

"You got him involved in this, Tommy. I coded twice in the ICU because of you. That means I died twice. You are the one who sicked him on me." I shouted

"I know, and I'm so sorry, Makayla." He said.

"Sorry doesn't cut it, how on earth can you claim to love me doing all this to me, and more, and sicking your dog, Gabe, on me. I was nearly raped, Tommy. I nearly died. You are a coward, just like Gabe." I screamed.

"Who killed my car battery and unlocked all my doors," I demanded.

"That was me," he admitted.

"And what about cutting off all my hair?"

"That was Gabe, Makayla. Another dick move of his. I would never ruin your beautiful hair. But after I punched Gabe for doing that, he said it was to make me less attractive to other guys. But you are still beautiful with short hair." He continued, "I killed your car battery though, I needed your attention."

"So, you and Gabe both found me at the lake and stalked me there, too?" I asked.

"Yes, he answered. We followed one of your friends' boyfriends and his friends and found your trailer and Shooters 21 where you worked." He said.

"Was that Gabe or you that destroyed my room?" I asked.

"We decided we needed you to pay attention to me." He answered.

"So, you both broke in and knocked my closets over, twice, and destroyed my room and wrote that horrible message above my bed?" I asked. "That was both of us." He said it like it was nothing. "We wanted to have a little fun scaring you."

"You're a punk!" I screamed at him.

"Gabe was getting more and more into scaring and stalking you. He took your stuff. I didn't know he had taken anything until later when he showed it to me. He said he was keeping it. I told him that wasn't part of the plan, and if he kept doing his own thing, our partnership would be over."

"PARTNERSHIP? Are you kidding? Is that what it was? You both taking turns ruining my life?" I shouted.

"And who put the razor blades on my car door handle when I was living at the lake, and sent me black roses, and left that disturbing note on my car?" I asked.

"That was me, and I'm so sorry, Makayla. I saw you with Levi, who Gabe was supposed to have killed, dancing at the Tiki bar after whoring yourself out to a bachelor, and I got really angry," he said. "I regret doing that, Makayla, please forgive me."

I rubbed the back of my fingers and felt the scars.

I wanted to scream, *Hell no I don't forgive you*, but I was going to need him to believe that maybe there was still a chance for us, so I needed to quit screaming at him. Then maybe he would let down his guard, and he could take off the zip ties. I need to calm down and soften up or I'm never getting out of here.

I needed to manipulate him. So, I said, "I forgive you, Tommy" I barely choked out. "I can see how that would be hard to see, but you shouldn't have gotten mad enough to hurt me so badly." I said.

"Tommy, why are you calling me Makayla now? You've always called me Mac." I asked. He said, "because we are starting over. You have a new look and a new name. Mac doesn't sound as beautiful as Makayla does." He answered.

"I was just mad you wouldn't stop seeing Levi, but Gabe was becoming obsessed with you. He kept going on and on about the things we should do to you to get your attention. He didn't love you like I do, he was just obsessed. I should have put a bullet in him when he took your stuff, but I still needed him to follow you." He replied.

"I can understand that." I lied. "You can?" Tommy asked, surprised.

"Yes, kind of. It doesn't make sense to me, but I see how it made sense to you." I answered. And who came into the bathroom while I was in the shower and moved everything around and put my clothes in the living room."

Tommy sighed. "That was me. When I came into the bathroom, I wanted to pull you out of the shower and make love with you right then. I wanted you so badly. You have no idea how hard it was to leave the bathroom with you in it. You were so close to me, and naked. Then maybe you would remember how much you loved me. I kept thinking, maybe if I just made love to you, you'd know. But I decided to stick to the plan of stalking you and scaring you. It was kind of revenge for me at that point."

"So let me get this straight. You and Gabe stalked me and killed my ex and tried to kill my current boyfriend, Levi?" I asked but Tommy interrupted me. He said, "Quit saying his name,"

Tommy yelled. " "He is no longer your boyfriend," Tommy snarled.

"OK, so you and Gabe did everything you did because you wanted to have a conversation with me? That makes no sense." I stated. "Well, let's have it," I said. "Let's have this conversation that you so desperately needed to have with me." I said irritably.

Then Tommy said, "scaring you and stalking you was what you deserved after how cruel you were to me when you broke up with me." Then I said, "You think I was cruel? Seriously? What about everything you did to me when we were together? That was way crueler, and that is why I broke up with you." I snapped back.

He said he was sorry. He said this time it will be different. That he had changed.

This time? Did he seriously think there would be a next time?

I had to make him believe that there might be a next time. That was going to be hard seeing I couldn't stand even looking at him.

Cool your jets, Mac I said to myself, trying to keep my composure.

I kept rubbing my wrists and making it very obvious, and purposely squealed under my breath hoping he would take them off.

"Are those too tight, Makayla?" He asked. "Yes," I answered. "Here, I'll loosen them," he said. "Can you please just take them off? I'm not going anywhere, and the floor is damp and cold. Could I please sit on that cot over there?" I asked pointing to the cot.

He looked at me for a while, deciding whether or not to trust me, and I kept eye contact with him, as hard as that was, while making a pleading look. He reached into his pocket and pulled out his large pocket knife and opened it. He started walking over to me and told me I better not try anything. I told him I wouldn't.

I told him I still wanted to understand why he did all those hurtful things he did. He cut the zip ties and helped me off the ground.

"Tommy," I asked, "I need my medication." He told me not to worry, he brought my medication with him, but he wasn't giving it to me because he liked the "raw" Makayla." I was woozy from the drug he injected me with. He helped me to the cot, and I sat down.

"What did you inject me with? I feel so woozy," I asked him. "Is it safe with lithium?" I asked. He said it was a roofie from a friend, but three times the dose. "What?" I asked in disbelief. "That could have killed me," I said. "I tried it out on a few people first, Makayla, including Gabe, I would never hurt you." he said. "But you did," I said, showing him the scars on the back of my fingers.

He lowered his head. "I told you I was sorry, and you said you forgave me." He said slowly lifting his head as he spoke those words and getting angry with me.

"You're right," I said. "I do forgive you, but you did hurt me, and you just said you never would." I responded.

He walked over to me, this time he used handcuffs, but he cuffed only one wrist to the frame of the cot and angrily stomped up the stairs. Then I heard the door open and close upstairs. Then a car engine fired up. He's leaving! OK, he just did one cuff on one wrist. I tried pulling, I looked to see if I could slip the cuff off the cot, but it was a no go. I pulled and pulled then I heard Tommy over the Ring doorbell.

"STOP!" he screamed.

"Don't make me come back and cuff both your hands." I told him I was sorry, I just wanted to walk around. And nothing.

Crickets.

My wrist was now bleeding. I lay there thinking of Levi. I thought about my parents, my sister, and my friends. They all must be so worried right now. I can't bear the thought of never seeing them again.

Then I felt something sharp under the mattress. Moving as little as possible, I lifted the side of the mattress, and there was a small piece of the metal frame that was nearly broken off. Once the sun was down and he only had night vision and was probably asleep, I was going to break it off the rest of the way, so I had a weapon.

"How am I going to get out of this one?" I asked myself under my breath.

Ugh. I just needed to keep him talking. Keep being me but show that I'm hearing him, that's what he's wanted all along, my attention. Maybe that will get me bonus points and he'll let me out of this basement.

The lock on the door was a deadbolt. The key side was facing me. And I'm pretty sure there is a combination or a padlock and latch on the outside of the door. I could hear the click, and then a latch both when he came in and when he left.

Crap!

I have to earn his trust to get out of here. Where did he go anyway? I was exhausted not just from the abduction but the drugs he gave me. I laid down on the cot. The metal was freezing. I saw a blanket folded at the end of the cot, and I tried to reach for it, but couldn't grab it. I used my toes to scrunch it up and then pulled it towards me until I could reach it.

Score!

I covered up, trying to get warm. Once I was covered, I let my body go limp and relax.

God's got this, I thought, *So I've got this!* With that, I drifted off to sleep.

Chapter 16: The Search Continues

Mac's parents landed and they got Michelle's message. They called Michelle immediately and said that they had made it back. They were obviously very upset about Mac's abduction. Mac's mom was just crying because she didn't understand because the stalker was dead.

That's what we all thought. I can't imagine what they are going through. I could a little I guess, seeing I'm going through it too. I kept thinking about the worst-case scenarios. But I kept reminding myself that I taught Mac a lot, and she can hold her own. But if she's drugged up, I'm not sure how well she can use those skills.

There was a knock on the door. It was Officer John and a couple of officers. They wanted to try and piece together a timeline from when Mac was abducted a few hours earlier, but he didn't have any updates. We were all talking about the situation when Officer John told everyone to be quiet. What's going on? I thought. He was listening to the police scanner.

"Mac has been spotted," he yelled so we all could hear.

We all rushed over to him to listen to the police scanner. He was generous and let us. There were several reports of a young lady with short brown hair, about 5'9 or 5'10, that at a stop light crawled out of the trunk of a red, four-door sedan, waving down cars and running.

Yes, Mac, *keep fighting him, and we'll find you!*

"I think we have enough for an Amber alert," Officer John said. We kept listening, it said then the driver grabbed her. They said a few men got out of their vehicles to stop him, but Tommy had a gun and fired a round in the air, so they backed off.

A couple of videos were submitted which they were going to put on the news. Then witnesses said he put her back in the trunk and sped off headed to the highway. The plates are registered to a Tommy Baxter.

"Didn't they already clear him as a suspect? "I asked.

"Tommy?" Mac's mom said. "How did I not see this coming?"

We kept listening, the final police scanner update was a suspect, Tommy Baxter, he is driving a red four- door sedan with blacked out windows, Missouri license plate number 12X5GG and he is approximately six feet tall, he has a goatee, short brown hair, blue eyes, and a fit build. He's reported as wearing a black shirt and dark jeans with athletic shoes. He is to be considered armed and dangerous. Do not approach, call the tip's hotline, 1-888-FOR-TIPS.

Officer John told another officer that we needed all this information out to the news and press as soon as possible. He told him to put out an alert to the public and all law enforcement within a 60-mile radius and start an Amber alert. The officer ran off to do what he was told.

Mac's mom fell to her knees and started praying. We all joined her, Michelle, Mac's dad, and myself. We were all praying for a safe return and that Mac hasn't been harmed and also praising God that as of now, she's fighting and she's alive. Mac's mom grabbed my hand and said, "Levi, please feel welcome to stay here so you can stay informed too." "Thank you," I said, "I appreciate that, and I will." I said with a smile. "Good," she replied. "Mac loves you so much, and I know you love her too," she said.

Suddenly, everyone's phones were screaming. It was an Amber alert; it was for Mac. *"Makayla Jackson, last seen wearing a light-colored blouse and jeans, 18-years-old, short brown hair. She's 5'10 with green eyes and a fit build. Abductor is Tommy Baxter, last seen wearing a black shirt and jeans and athletic shoes and possibly a ball cap in Warrensburg, MO headed towards 50 highway in a red four-door sedan. Makayla may not be visual. He is armed and dangerous so do not approach, call law enforcement right away if you see the abductor or the victim. The tips hot line is 1-888-FOR-TIPS. Makayla was last seen being put into the trunk...."*

I hated just waiting. I wanted to search for her. Maybe that profiler could help us figure out where she might be. He said before a secluded area and the police had gone knocking on doors and came up empty. At least there were areas to rule out so they could find her faster.

There was a knock at the door. Mac's mom went to answer the door, and it was Mandi. She gave her a big hug, and Mandi said she got the Amber alert for Mac and asked if there were any updates on where Mac was. I got up off the couch, and she gave me a hug. We all sat back down, and I filled her in.

She was crying. "Mac's a fighter!" she said. "She managed to get out of his trunk. I just can't believe Tommy was behind all of this the whole time. He was a total crybaby when she broke things off with him. This makes no sense. Or maybe it does, seeing he had help." she said. "I agree," I said. "Do you guys mind if I hang out here with you all while they search for Mac?" Mandi asked. "Of course not," Mac's mom said." The more the better. We are all pulling for her.

"She's smart, and she knows how to manipulate people, we all know that. Not in a wrong way, you know what I mean. So, she can do the same with Tommy. She is strong physically and mentally. She is going to save herself, just wait and see. God's got her now. She can't lose." Mac's mom said.

"I thought I could sit here and wait, but I can't. I'm going to go to the secluded areas here in town and see if I can find his car or see anything suspicious." I announced.

"Be careful," Mandi said. Then Mac's dad, Derek, grabbed his gun. "I'm coming with you," he announced. "I'll drive," I said.

Derek grabbed a few things, and we were off. I drove to the spot where Mac was last reported as being seen.

"What do you think, Sir?" I asked Mac's dad. He said, "call me, Derek." "Which way do you think we should head, Derek?" I asked. "Let's go towards the highway. Once we take the next exit, there are a lot of secluded farm homes the police never covered. It's about 20 minutes from here." He said, "Ok then, Derek, let's do this," I said. I headed towards the highway, it wasn't far at all.

We were on the highway for about five minutes when Derek told me to take an exit. I could barely see it. I guess it was more like a turn than an exit. It was a bumpy country road. I slowed down to not give away that we were there. I found a tree line to hide the Jeep. Derek and I agreed that we should go on foot. Derek was going to cover the south side, and I would cover the north side. He brought an extra gun but didn't tell anyone.

"You know how to shoot?" He asked me. "Yes, Sir," I said. He handed me a pistol with two clips. "It's loaded," he said. I thanked him, and I put a bullet in the chamber and put the safety on, then Derek gave me a walkie-talkie since our cell service was bad. We tested them and then we went our separate ways. "Make sure you radio me before you try and get closer to a house so I will know where you are in case he gets to you too. The last thing we need is you in the ICU again or worse!" Derek said. I agreed and told him to do the same. Then we turned to our directions and started walking.

I saw several farm homes, but they were all about a mile or more apart.

I'm going to be doing a lot of walking, I thought to myself. Then, I approached the first house. It was huge. "Derek, I'm approaching a farm home closest to my car. I'm going to look for a red car." I said. "OK, sounds good, be safe," Derek said.

I didn't see a red car outside the house, but the house had a large garage. It had windows, so I looked inside. No red car. Then I heard a shotgun load. "What are you doing here? Get off my property." the homeowner said. I put up my hands and turned around. I said, "Have you seen the news sir, about a girl that was abducted?" "Yes," he answered. "She's not here." he replied.

"I'm her boyfriend, and her dad and I are searching the remote areas because the intel we have is that she would be somewhere secluded." I said. "I haven't seen anything," he said, lowering his shotgun. "Shouldn't the cops be doing this?" He asked. "The police are doing the best they can, but they never covered this area so we thought instead of sitting around, waiting on word about Mac, we'd check some homes ourselves." I responded.

"I hope you find her. I saw the video on the news where he just shoved her in the trunk." He said, "I will call the tips line if I see a red sedan at all." He promised. "Thank you, sir, and I'm sorry I was snooping. The fact is she could be anywhere. I was looking in your garage to see if there was a red car." I said. "No worries, I hope you find her, unfortunately, I'm not familiar with the other people who live out here, but hopefully she is in one of them, or they saw something suspicious," he said. I thanked him, and I started the mile-long walk to the next house.

As I approached the next home, I radioed Derek about the first house and that I was at the second house. He wasn't having any luck either.

This home was smaller. Like a cottage. I noticed the garage didn't have windows. I took my chances and knocked on the door.

The owner opened the door and asked me what I wanted. He was pretty rude. He probably thought I was a solicitor. "Hello, Sir." I said. "I am looking for my girlfriend who was abducted. The profiler on her case said she's in a secluded area, so her father and I are going door to door in this area to see if anyone has seen anything." I said. "Are you talking about the girl from the news?" He asked, "Yes," I answered. He softened up.

"That poor girl. She's been through so much and is now abducted. The world we live in." He said. He proceeded to tell me that he hadn't seen a sign of them or a red sedan. So, I told him thank you, and I would move on to the next house. He wished me luck and said he was praying for her safe return. I told him I appreciated that. He went back inside, and I radioed Derek. "I've cleared two houses, how about you?" I asked. He said to hold on for a minute.

Is he on to something?

I started walking to the next house, which was also about a mile away. Then I heard Derek on the radio. He said he had cleared one house and was on the way to the next one. "Have you seen anything suspicious yet?" I asked him. "No," he said. "We'll have to come back and clear East and West." He said. "Sounds good." I said. "I'm halfway to my third house and, I think, the last house." I told him. He said to keep him posted. I told him I would.

I was getting winded, the uneven grass was making this walk much harder than the track I walk and run on. Three miles on the track is nothing. I was slowly getting to the next house, I stopped when I was close just to take in the house and surrounding area.

This was a log cabin with gardening and was pretty much a homestead. There were chickens in the backyard. I saw a goat and three horses. I doubt this is the place, but you never know. I remembered Mac telling me how much she loved horseback riding.

Where are you, Mac?

I approached the home. They had a four-car garage, with windows. I quietly walked by them on my way to the front door and peeked inside. No red sedan.

Damn

I knocked on the door, but no one answered. I rang the doorbell. A few moments later a lady, probably in her 60's, answered the door. "What can I do for you?" she asked. "Have you seen the news about an abducted female in a red sedan?" She said, "Yes." I continued, "Well, I'm her boyfriend and her dad and I are knocking on the doors trying to see if anyone has seen anything.

"That poor girl," she said. "I'm sorry, but I don't know anything and haven't seen anything either," she responded. "OK," I said. "Thank you for your time," and I left. She yelled after me, "I hope you find her!" "Me too," I replied. I didn't see any more homes in this direction.

I wanted to drive the car a little further North to see if there were more homes. I radioed Derek, "Have you found anything? Do you have more houses?" He radioed back, "No, nothing. There are no more homes or structures." He said. "OK," I said back, "let's both head to the Jeep. I'm about three miles away." I said. "Same here," he said. We both started making our way to the Jeep.

We both were worn out, but we decided to drive further into the countryside to see if more houses existed. Both North and South. There were a few. So, we decided to head home and rest a bit, but it was getting dark, so we decided to hit further North and South again tomorrow, and together so we didn't have to walk so much. We would go further North first, then farther South. If we didn't find anything, then we would do East and West of that tree line and hide my car again, the next day.

When we got home everyone looked so hopeful. Then we had to tell them we came up empty, but we were going to rest, and then go back and look further North and South tomorrow when we had daylight. If we came up empty, we would do East and West after that. "You'll find her, I just know it." Krista said. Mac's parents wanted me to call them by their first names, but it was so odd for me. I was raised to say Sir and Ma'am. But sometimes I would slip their names, but it felt natural.

Derek and I rested while Krista made sandwiches for us, and some fruit, and lots of water. "Thank you so much, ma'am," I said as I was accepting the plate of food.

Crap, I did it again.

"I meant, Krista." She laughed. She said, "I'm good with either, Levi. Now eat up!" "I can definitely do that." I replied.

Chapter 17: Imprisoned

When I woke up, I was still cuffed to the cot frame. I saw some prepacked food next to the cot. A bunch of crap food. Pastries individually wrapped, but some real food too like granola bars, and canned fruit and vegetables with a can opener. Gross, I thought.

Wait a minute, I thought, *I can use the can tops after I open them. They are sharp!!*

Yes, I have a weapon. I just have to hide it and not let me be seen in the Ring camera. Too bad I'm not zip tied. Then I could cut the ties. I definitely can not cut through this cuff!

I opened the canned peaches first. I liked them. Then I slid the top under the cot mat. I dipped my fingers in and pulled out the peaches. I was starving. I ate the whole can. "Tommy," I screamed so he could hear me. "Just a minute," he replied from the ring camera. Then I heard footsteps down the stairs.

"What do you need?" He asked. I said, "A few things. Could you please open the curtains on the windows. It's so dark in here and it's depressing. Also, I need to be able to wash my hands and drain the cans." I requested.

"I need the bathroom and a shower. But I can't with this cuff on. And I don't want you watching me." I said.

He said if I promise not to try something, he will take the cuff off my wrist so I could go to the bathroom and drain the cans. He said he'd bring me a trash can as well as some napkins. I thanked him, and he removed the cuff. I rubbed my wrist, and Tommy saw the blood. He said he'd grab a first aid kit as well.

After he went upstairs to get everything, I drained the peaches can, then washed my hands. Thankfully, there was toilet paper, so I used the bathroom, praying he wasn't watching the entire time. I had to pee so bad.

I washed my hands again and went back to the cot. I got back up and I walked over to the Ring and rang the bell. "What, Makayla?" He said. "I also need a towel to get a shower, two towels if that's alright." I responded. He said he'd bring that down too. I felt so gross and needed a shower. I have no idea how long I've been here. I thought it might have been two days, but I wasn't sure.

Suddenly I heard a seriously loud alarm upstairs. It was an Amber Alert! PLEASE let that be for me.

"SHIT!" I heard Tommy scream from upstairs. That must be for me! Then I heard him yelling profanities and stomping around. *YES!* I thought to myself. I was all smiles.

A few minutes later Tommy came back to the door. Before he opened it, I heard the click and latch scraping the metal it was attached to. Yep, he definitely had a lock on the outside too. Then he opened the door.

He just stared at me. He said, "There is an Amber alert out for you. My full name and description were on it. How am I supposed to work now, Makayla?" I paused. "I'm so sorry Tommy. I don't know your financial situation." I said

Then he said, "We are going to have to move out of state. I don't know where but I'm not having someone else watch over you after what Gabe did." He said. "Thank you," I replied.

"We need new names. I have a guy that can do that. As soon as I reach him, we will go." He stated.

Then he got the first aid kit and bandaged my wrist. I asked if he would leave the kit so after my shower I could re-bandage it. He said he would. Then he gave me another blanket. He said I looked cold the other night.

He was watching me sleep. Psycho. I thought.

But I said, "Thank you, yes, it's very cold down here." Then he gave me two towels and set some napkins on the floor with my food. "I totally forgot you need water, Makayla," he said, "I'll be right back." And he left. I didn't hear the click this time. I went to the door and tried to open it. It wouldn't budge.

The deadbolt he put on was pretty heavy duty. I walked around because I knew he was watching me. I was stretching my legs. I really needed to walk around. But of course, as I did, I was looking for a way to escape.

Unfortunately, the door was my only option. I had to get him to trust me and let me out of the basement, without the zip ties. Maybe when he brings me up to leave the state. God, please let me escape before that, I prayed. That was the only way. Unless he somehow forgets to lock the door. I wasn't holding my breath on that one.

Then the door opened, and Tommy came down with a case of bottled water, and it was cold too. "Thank you, Tommy." I said. He smiled and said I needed to stay hydrated. "We have a long day ahead of us," he said. "My guy is coming today to get our papers and new identification."

"Question is, can you ride up front and behave, or will you ride to another state in the trunk?" He asked. I said, "I won't try anything."

Yea, right, I thought.

I asked him again for my meds, but he said no. "I want to see the real you off all these meds, remember?" He asked. "I want to see you the way you were when we were together."

I hadn't taken my meds for several days and I was struggling.

I told him, "I might have a manic or depressive episode without it. And it was a drug I had to wean off of or I could get extremely depressed or have a huge manic episode. Either the kind of manic episode where I feel like I'm on cloud nine and no one could touch me, or extremely angry and go off on you since you are the only one around, and I don't want to do that to you."

After explaining that to Tommy he said he'd start weaning me off it. He went upstairs and grabbed my meds. He brought them down to me in my pill box. All my meds cut in half. He said next week he would cut them in half again.

Next week! I screamed in my head.

I was so pissed. I didn't need a manic or depressive episode right now. I decided tomorrow to fake being very depressed. I stayed on the cot the rest of the day. I cried, so Tommy could hear it in the Ring, and only got up to use the bathroom. I didn't eat either, which was hard.

Tommy came down with another gentleman. He was shorter than Tommy, and a tad overweight. He and Tommy talked and then identification papers were in front of me to sign. Also, he needed a picture of me.

He brought a selfie light stick with him. Then Tommy told me to put on some makeup and handed me a bag filled with makeup. I hesitated, but he meant business. So, I went into the bathroom where a small handheld mirror was. Ugh. I couldn't do my make up this way! But I figured it out. Next, they made me pose for a picture. I did hesitantly. And they left. I have to get out of here before he makes me go out of state.

Tommy came down to check on me the next evening. "You've been in bed since yesterday afternoon. It's evening now and you haven't left your cot." He stated. I told him, "I'm just really tired. Maybe a little depressed. Could you close the curtains." I asked. Tommy said no, I needed the light if I was depressed. Then Tommy opened all the curtains.

Yes, manipulation number one is a success! Curtains are open!

Then he said, "I'm so sorry, Makayla. I heard you cry most of the day today, and a little yesterday," he said. "Is it the decrease in medication causing you to be depressed?" He asked.

I told him, "I don't know, and I don't really care. You are going to kill me anyway, right? So, just do it now and let it be over with. Just please let me write a letter to my parents first. Then do what you brought me here to do." I said with fake tears.

Tommy said, "Makayla, I would never kill you, I'm not going to kill you, Makayla, I would never kill you, I am going to give you your meds as prescribed. I won't cut those. I didn't realize how much you needed them. Just give me a few minutes to figure it out. Or do you remember the dosage?" I told him I take 300 mg in the morning, and 600 mg at night" Then he left to get my full dosage of Lithium.

Manipulation number two, I'm winning. Poor depressed Mac.

I'll keep manipulating him until I get out of this basement. I decided the peach lid wasn't going to help me escape so I used it for manipulation number three.

I cut the palm of my hand. It hurt but I had to make a point to Tommy who supposedly loved me. Tommy returned with the remaining pills for my bipolar disorder. I purposely refused to take it. I was going to do a little more manipulation. I was moving my hand and made sure Tommy would see the cut and all the blood.

"What happened to your hand?" Tommy said looking at my hand. "What the hell did you do, Makayla," he asked. I told him, "Just leave me alone," He insisted I tell him. "When I get really depressed sometimes I self-mutilate to make myself feel better. But it didn't work." I said.

"Shit," Tommy said. "You need stitches, Makayla."

He looked through the first aid kit and found sterile strips that work like stitches. He applied them to the palm of my hand after he cleaned it up and sanitized it. Then he wrapped gauze around my hand to keep it clean. "You will feel better soon if you take your meds," Tommy said. I acted reluctant for a moment, then I took the pills that he held back.

"See," I said, "there is no 'raw Mac'. My bipolar got bad really quickly. I'm just a shell or a psycho without my meds, but what's the point? You are just going to end up killing me, like Gabe tried."

Manipulation number three! Poor depressed Mac is hurting herself!

He apologized and said," I didn't think it was that bad, and Makayla, I would never kill you. I love you." He reminded me why I had a reason to live. He said that we still had so much to do together. We were leaving the state as soon as I felt better. We would be back together soon, to hold on to that and remember, you have your whole life with me to look forward to.

That alone is enough to make me want to kill myself.

Then he asked, "How long will it take to get you back to normal." I said, "I have no idea, and I don't care." He said we wouldn't leave the state until I was feeling better. So, I plan on not being better until I can figure out how to escape.

Then Tommy said, "I know after some time, you will love me again like you used to. We just need to talk through it all, and this was the only way to get your attention. Your full attention, so we can talk through everything. I know I'm the one who screwed it up for the most part."

"Can I just go back to sleep, please, after I use the restroom?" I asked. "Yes," he said. "Let me bring you some more pillows and blankets. I was assembling a twin bed from upstairs for you to sleep on instead of this cot. I'll finish it after you get a nap." He said

"That is so sweet of you," I replied. "Or could you leave it upstairs and let me sleep up there. The mold and mildew are making me itch and it smells. I feel like I'm suffocating. I'm allergic to mold. Not enough for an Epi pen, but I itch like crazy. I even get bad migraines from it." I told him.

"I'll think about it." He said and he left. Well, I'm stuck in this cot for a few days so he doesn't try to cut my meds again. I needed a clear head, and I don't think he wants to hurt me. Two or three days passed, with Tommy checking on me like three times a day. He kept apologizing for cutting my meds.

And I kept up the 'depressed' charade. I had asked for more tissues because they were almost all gone from me wiping my eyes and blowing my nose. It was easy to cry, I just thought about my parents and Levi, and the waterworks came. More to manipulate him with.

Banging and an electric screwdriver woke me up. I looked behind me and Tommy had the twin bed built. "You woke me up," I told him. "I'm sorry Makayla. I thought maybe a nice comfy bed might help you to feel better faster," Tommy said as he was making the bed.

"Thank you, Tommy," I said. When he finished, he helped me walk to the twin bed and then brought all my stuff over. "I feel so gross. I need a shower but I'm too tired," I told him "And I don't want you watching me." I told him. He said "I wouldn't watch,

Makayla." Yea right, I thought. I had to pee again, so I asked Tommy to turn around, and I went to the bathroom. I washed my hands and then I went back to the twin bed Tommy put together, and I laid down and cried, keeping up my depressed facade.

The next day, after faking I was depressed for three days, and I've been held captive I think for four days. I decided to get up. I yelled for Tommy on the Ring bell he had set up. "Hey Makayla, you are up." He said, "are you feeling better?" he asked. "Yes," I said. "I need to take a shower though, but first, I'm seriously craving a donut. Would you mind getting me one?" I asked. There was a long pause. "Sure, anything for you, Makayla. I am so happy you are feeling better," he said. I figured the more he got out, the more likely he would get spotted.

Manipulation number four! Get him out in the public so he gets spotted!

I asked him if he was going to watch me shower. He promised he wouldn't. I thanked him. I told him, "I don't want you to see me naked, yet, and I have some PTSD from the break in the bathroom while I was in the shower. I'm begging you not to watch." I said, and I made him swear he wouldn't, and he told me again he wouldn't. "OK then, I'll get a shower now while you get donuts. And I thanked him again."

He told me I have a suitcase of fresh clothes under the cot. I thanked him for that. I heard the front door open and close and his engine start and heard the gravel as he pulled out.

Then, with huge hesitation, I took a shower. It felt so good. He had all my shower stuff in there. I took a steaming hot shower and then saw that the glass all around the shower was completely fogged over! Awesome I thought, he couldn't watch me if he wanted to. Next time I'll start the shower before I get undressed.

After my shower, I wrapped my body in one of the towels and used the other towel for my hair. I pulled out the suitcase and found some panties and my bra. I put them on and then grabbed a shirt and a pair of jeans and socks. I didn't see any shoes.

I rang the Ring doorbell and a few seconds later, he answered. "What's up, Makayla?" "Can you bring in my shoes from out of your trunk when you get back. The floor down here is so hard and cold." I said. He said he would. He just got to the donut place, he said. "I'll be back in a bit," he said, then it was quiet. A donut really did sound good.

After about 30 minutes he was back, I could hear the gravel. Then I heard his car door shut and the front door open. I heard him come down the stairs. He handed me a box of donuts, and my shoes, still tied together. I opened the box, and all my favorite donuts were in there. I forced a smile, and said, "Thank you so much, Tommy. That means so much to me. You remembered my favorites. Thank you." "You're welcome, Makayla. I remember everything about you, because I'm in love with you. Soon you will be in love with me again." He said smiling. He grabbed a donut and sat down next to me on the bed and we ate the donuts together. Yuck. I wish he would just leave.

After my second donut, I started feeling woozy. What is going on, I thought. Oh my gosh, he drugged me, but why? I shouted in my head. I asked Tommy, "Why did you drug me? I can feel it, I'm getting woozy." "I thought it might perk you up a bit after being depressed for so long," Tommy said. "NO!" I screamed, "You just set me back again," I screamed at him. "Get out of here and leave me alone," I cried. "It won't last long, Makayla," he said. I just need you to sleep for a bit." "I've been sleeping for days." I said. "Wait! Are you going to do something to me." I asked. "Why do you need me asleep?" He didn't answer. He just kept eating his donut. "Answer me," I screamed at him. "Are you going to do something to me?" I demanded.

He said no, and I didn't believe him one bit. I threw the box of donuts across the basement. "You just ruined any trust I had for you, Tommy, just leave" I said as I started falling asleep. I went to where I woke up the first time, next to the drainpipe, and leaned against it and the wall. I was crying so hard. "I can't believe you don't trust me now, Tommy," I said crying. "Don't touch me!" I yelled. Then I drifted off and it was lights out.

I woke up covered up in the twin bed Tommy put together. I had no idea how long I'd been out. He wasn't there, and he moved the bed closer to the ring camera and the cot was gone. I was still really woozy. I got up and tried walking around. I stumbled a lot. I also stumbled upon another camera. It was small and round and in the corner of one of the windows. "Has that always been here?" I asked myself out loud. Or is that why he needed me to sleep? I wondered.

I grabbed it and threw it across the basement. Next thing I knew Tommy was downstairs. "You had another camera on me all this time?" I asked him, screaming. "Or is that why you wanted me asleep?" I demanded. "You are ruining any chance of me trusting you, or even liking you at this point, let alone fall back in love with you," I shouted at him.

"OK, Makayla, you said your bipolar could make you angry and you take it out on others, and since I'm the only one here it's me." Tommy stated. That pissed me off so bad. "No, I'm just a human being held captive, I'm not having a bipolar flare up!" I shouted. "Here are your meds, Makayla," Tommy said. I took them with some water in the water bottle. "I'm never eating anything you bring me from upstairs ever again," I said. He said if he wants to drug me, he could do it with a syringe. "I'm in control here, Makayla," he said. I just looked away and wouldn't talk to him at all.

Stop, I told myself.

Now, how am I going to get him to trust me after that flip-out. I asked myself. Ugh

Chapter 18: The Great Escape

I worked on the knot in my shoes. It was a tough one, but I got them united and put them on.

Tommy opened the door and asked how I was feeling. "Better, I think" I said. "Good." he replied. "I'm really sorry I flipped out on you, Tommy. It's not my fault, I swear. My bipolar disorder can be really bad." I choked out. I did not want to apologize for any of it, but I needed his trust and him to believe we stood a chance.

He leaned in to kiss me.

I wanted to vomit but I needed to seduce him and make sure he was buying my act of loving him again. I kissed him back just like I did before when I was afraid to break up with him.

Faking it.

He said, "kiss me again, like you mean it. That's the test. I'll be able to tell by your kiss if you love me and mean it or not." So, I did. I gave him a deep long kiss like we used to. I still wanted to vomit. He said, "That's more like it. But I don't fully trust you yet, Makayla."

"I understand," I said. "Just please, I don't want my first time to be in a smelly and cold basement. Can we go upstairs to your bed, when it's time?" I asked looking deep into his eyes, even though that made me sick to my stomach. Just like kissing him did.

I thought I would just pretend I was kissing Levi, but I couldn't. I couldn't taint that connection with Levi.

"I thought you were saving yourself for marriage, Makayla?" he asked. "What changed?" "I don't know," I said. "Maybe because I'm older now and no one waits before marriage anymore, I'm still not sure I'm ready. I guess it depends on how good you are to me, and if I feel safe with you, and feel I can fall in love with you again," I said. I'm still not sure so don't count on it though, OK? I asked him.

"I can understand that," he said. "I know I scared you for a long time, but it's over." He said. Like I could ever feel safe with him after what he and Gabe did to me. I tried not to think of it. "I want to feel safe with you, but it's hard after what happened, and now being locked up in your basement." I said, "And won't your parents wonder what you are doing?" I asked. His head dropped.

I heard him sniffle. He stayed quiet. "Tommy, what did I say, why are you so upset, babe?" "You just called me babe, Makayla." He said, "Oh, I'm sorry, I won't do it again if it upsets you." "No," he said, "I really like it."

He said he was upset because I asked about his parents. They were both killed in a car accident one year ago. I told him I was so sorry. Both of his parents were awesome, kind, loving, accepting, and a million other things. He said thank you and then grabbed me and hugged me and he hugged me hard.

I actually do feel a bit sorry for him right now. But I've got to figure out how I'm going to get upstairs. He finally let me go and he said he was going to make us dinner. He was going to make Chinese. My favorite. "You still know me so well," I said. I had no plans to eat dinner with him. I decided to open the can of pears and use the lid to make my escape when Tommy came down with dinner.

Both his hands would be full, and I could cut him and run past him in the doorway, that was the plan anyway. I smelled the Chinese and it smelled good. But freedom smells better.

I heard Tommy coming down the stairs, and he fumbled with the lock. He opened the door, and I stood there. I pulled out the sharp lid from the can, and I wrapped paper towels around the side I'd be holding. I also managed to get a somewhat sharp piece of metal off the cot I slept on. I hid it in my suitcase. I made sure I had that, along with the can lid.

He never saw it coming. He thought I went to the door to help him.

Idiot.

"It's ready, Makayla," he said. Then I grabbed my weapon, and I sliced his arm. He dropped the food, and I stabbed him from behind with the metal from the cot and I ran upstairs. I was unlocking the front door when I felt Tommy grab me.

He slammed me against the wall and put his hands around my neck and was choking me. I couldn't breathe. He tried to kiss me, and I turned my head. He put more pressure around my neck.

I put what Levi taught me into action, and I grabbed both his middle fingers with each hand and I pulled them hard and fast toward the back of his hand. I heard a disturbing crack, and he let go and cried out. I didn't even hesitate. Coughing and desperately needing air, I kicked him in between the legs and when he bent over, I grabbed the back of his head and quickly raised my knee as hard as I could while slamming his face into my knee, then I ran to the front door and opened it.

I think I broke his nose. He was screaming my name but his voice sounded funny, but I kept going without looking back. "You have nowhere to go, Makayla." he said. "Come back and I'll pretend this never happened." He said. Hell no I thought. I'm getting out of here.

It was so bright outside. The country air smelled so good. Outside was a desolate area. There wasn't a single home as far as I could see. I saw a tree line ahead. What's behind it I thought, running towards the trees. I figured at least I could hide somewhere. I heard Tommy scream my name again, he was outside now, but I kept running.

I was still running until I heard a gunshot, from a shotgun. I heard it echo all around me. I stopped dead in my tracks. I completely froze. Then I slowly turned around behind me towards Tommy. He stood there on the front steps, holding a shotgun, aimed at me. I slowly turned back around looking at the trees.

I can't freeze, I told myself. Would he really shoot me? I'd rather be shot than give into him and endure whatever he has planned for me. Can he even aim with two broken fingers? I decided to keep running again towards the trees as fast as I could. I heard the shotgun, and I ran faster.

"MAKAYLA!" He kept screaming and I was starting to hear defeat in his tone. He continued running after me, shotgun in hand. Common, run faster Mac, I coached myself, I need to get into the trees and find somewhere to hide. Where the hell was I?

He was getting closer and now his tone was angry. Like he was on an adrenaline rush. Well, so was I and I got a good head start. I was out of breath, but I had to keep going. I glanced back and I was starting to put more distance between us, but I needed more if I was going to find a place to hide. I ran faster, if that was even possible. More distance between us. Good, I thought. "Makayla!" he screamed again. He wasn't as loud now. I was almost there.

"Keep going, Mac." I told myself out loud.

I turned and glanced back to look, and I felt myself trip over a branch.

"Crap!"

Get up, get up off the ground already, Mac, RUN. I Screamed to myself.

I was up and running within seconds, then I felt Tommy grabbing me and he put his arm around my neck. His finger was disfigured. Yep, I broke it. I stopped in my tracks. He started pulling me back to the house, and I pulled out the piece of metal from the cot, and I stabbed him in the side, then I stabbed him again in the chest.

I didn't hesitate, I started running again. I heard the gun again. Good, that means he had to slow down to try a shot. I can't believe he's trying to kill me when he thinks he loves me and I love him. Just the thought of that made me sick. I was almost to the tree line when I heard a gunshot again, but it wasn't the same sound. It was a different gun!

Chapter 19: The Search

We reached the tree line, and I hid my Jeep, but closer to the East. Neither Derek nor I found anything looking North and South. We spent two days searching those directions. Derek looked exhausted. I'm sure he was. I was too.

But knowing we might find Mac got me energized. It must have for Derek too because he perked up. So, we both got out of the car with our guns and walkie talkies and wished each other luck.

I was going East, Derek decided, and he'd go West. I told him I would leave the keys in the Jeep in case he needed them. I started walking farther East. I stayed in the tree line as long as I could so no one would see me. I saw a small farm house so I decided to approach it. I radioed Derek and let him know. "Be careful," he ordered. I knocked on the door, gun hidden, and this sweet old lady answered the door. She said, "so solicitors are coming this far out now? What are you selling?" she asked.

I told her I was just trying to find my girlfriend. "Really," she said. "Well, no one is here. This area is very secluded." I told her she was abducted so we were searching for any sign of her abductor. "Oh dear, that's horrible," she said. "I hope you find her!" "Thank you," I replied.

She invited me in for iced tea, and I accepted. I thought maybe she could point me in the direction of some other homes. We both sipped our iced teas, and she gave me the layout of the area. She said the nearest house in that direction was about two miles away. "Wow," I said.

"And who lives there?" I asked. She sipped more tea and said "I have no idea. They rarely leave the house, except for their son. His parents passed away about a year ago in a car accident, bless their souls, so he lives there alone. Forgive me," she said, "I forget his name." I told her that's OK. I asked, "does Tommy sound familiar?" "Yes," she replied. "That's it, Tommy." I was so excited, but I had to ask more questions.

Then I asked, "Do you know what color car he drives?" She said, "as a matter of fact I do. It's red. Not sure what type of car. My vision isn't the best these days, but it's red, I do know that."

"Thank you so much," I told her. "For the tea and the information, I have to go." I told her.

She wished me luck and I radioed Dereck and told him what she said. He said "go back in the tree line and stay there until I get there. It might take me 30 minutes but wait on me."

I told him I would wait and I headed to the tree line. I was just about to radio Derek that I was coming to get him in the Jeep, I heard gunshots. I radioed Derek and he heard them too. I told him I was headed there now. Then I started running to the house the old lady said a single man lived in and had a red car. It was definitely a good two miles. I was too far to go back to my Jeep. Every second counted with the gunshots.

I was running fast, faster than I'd ever ran. I saw Mac! She was just standing there and stopped running."

Mac, RUN

Then I saw her start running to the tree line. *That's my Mac, a fighter.* I fired off a shot to distract Tommy, and it worked. I was in the open and being shot at. Tommy was running after Mac. I shot at him again, but I missed, I was too far away. I kept running.

I radioed Derek and was barely able to talk. I was so out of breath. I told Derek, I found the house and I saw Mac. Tommy was shooting at her, but she was still running. I told him I fired off a few shots to distract Tommy. Derek, also out of breath, said he was nearing the Jeep. I turned around and I barely saw him in the distance. He was close to the Jeep, and I saw him going for it. He had a rifle so he could definitely get a good shot further away. I fired another shot at Tommy, then I had to change my clip. I looked back and I saw Derek driving towards us. A few moments later, he jumped out of the Jeep and immediately kneeled down to take the shot. Once in place, he fired.

Chapter 20: I'm Rescued

I heard Levi's voice, "Keep running, Mac!" he was screaming. So, I did. I heard gun fire exchange, and I ran faster.

Finally, I reached the tree line and it was dense. I ran deep into the forest line and then I stopped. I need to go back and get Levi! I couldn't run anymore, I needed to catch my breath. After I caught my breath, I ran probably a half-mile to the Jeep, that's when I first saw my dad, kneeling on the ground.

I hurried over so I could see what was going on, and that's when I saw the rifle.

Dad!

He was aiming at Tommy.

Take the shot, Dad! I screamed in my head.

Then I heard another shot, and it was echoing much louder than Tommy's gun. It was my dad's rifle. I looked at Tommy and he was hit. Then another shot, and Tommy fell to the ground.

My dad gave me a big hug, then we got in the Jeep and drove down to Tommy's house.

As we were driving, I saw Levi approach Tommy and he took his gun. Once there, I hopped out and gave him a big hug and a kiss. Tommy saw us kiss.

"See, Tommy, this is the man I love. He's a real man, he's good to me in ways you will never know. I love him and he loves me." I continued, "Oh, and this is for the razor blades on my door handle, and I kicked him as hard as I could right where he was shot, I had blood all over my shoe, but I didn't care. I leaned over Tommy as he started coughing up blood. "You are going to die right here, Tommy," I continued, "And no one is going to call an ambulance until you are dead," I said.

"What you did to me is unforgivable, Tommy. Everything you did to me and my loved ones, too. You and Gabe are both monsters. I hope you are right with God or you get right with him now." I said

Levi pulled me back, "That's enough, Mac. I know you will regret all of this later," he said. "No, I don't think I will on this one, I have plenty more to say, like kissing him, I nearly threw up." I said loudly so Tommy could hear me. "And every time you touched me and even heard your voice made my body shuddered," I kept going, "And taking me off my meds, like really. You aren't a doctor!" I screamed at him. You've set me back when I was even, you can't just not take your meds for days when you're bipolar." I screamed at him. "I'm lucky nothing major happened." I continued. "I faked being depressed to manipulate you, I did pretty good, didn't I?" I shouted. "I can't believe this is finally the end," I told Levi and my dad. "Oh, and this is for abducting me," I said as

I kicked his other gunshot wound. "There are so many reasons to keep kicking you. But I'm not that cruel. Unlike you." I said.

Levi pulled me back again and held me in his arms. I told my dad and Levi, "we should call an ambulance. Surely, I'll be safe when he's in jail. So, my dad got on his phone and he had a little service. And he made the call. "I can't believe I just said that," I told Levi. "Did you hear that Tommy," I shouted, "we are calling an ambulance for you."

"We aren't psychos like you and Gabe. Whether or not you live long enough to get help, it is up to God." I shouted.

Then Levi went to put pressure on his wounds. He told me to stay back. "Happy to." I said. "Here, I'll hold your gun." I told Levi. I went over to Tommy and I had the gun pointed at his head. "Just do it, " Tommy said, coughing up blood. "Don't tempt me." I said. "I wanted to be the one to kill you." I stated. "So maybe I will, except shooting someone who is helpless is something I can't do." I'm not disturbed, like you and Gabe.

Levi was still putting pressure on his wounds. When Levi looked at me, I saw Tommy reach under his back, then I heard the hammer snap. Levi heard it too and he stopped what he was doing and was inching away from him. I yelled to Levi, "watch out! Gun!" Tommy pulled out a pistol and aimed at Levi, I raised the gun and aimed at Tommy, and quickly I shot him in the chest two times. He went limp.

"Is he dead?" I asked Levi. "I think so," he said. "I'll check for a pulse," Levi said. He did and there wasn't a pulse. "I killed him." I said out loud. "It's over, for real this time," I said, crying. "You just saved my life, Mac," Levi said! "I love you," I told him.

"How did you find me?" I asked Levi and my dad. "We started searching secluded areas, and I came across this old lady down that way, she told me about this house and that he drove a red car, and that his name was Tommy" Levi said. "So, I headed this way and I saw you running, and Tommy was shooting his shotgun towards you, and you know the rest." He said.

Shortly, the police arrived, and Officer John was there. We were just barely still in his jurisdiction. He asked me if I was OK and if I needed medical attention. I told him that I was alright, I had a large cut and he drugged me the morning before, but I felt fine now. So, he had one of the paramedics look at my hand and wrist. They bandaged me up.

I told them everything that happened and what he did to me. I told them he drugged my food that morning, and I told him why he abducted me. He just wanted my full attention so we could talk. He thought we were going to work things out. He told me what all Gabe did and what he did in the stalking. Tommy killed Gabe because he saw on the news what he did to me. I told him he drugged me a couple times. I didn't know what with, and they said whatever he put in my donut that morning, is out of my system by now. I told them that Tommy was going to take me out of state.

Some guy came and took pictures for a new identification and forced me to sign some documents and I have no idea what they were.

The police needed us to stay to take our statements and the other officers were processing the scene and forensics were getting evidence from the crime scene. I told them everything from the front door of my home to my attempt to escape out of the trunk of his car, to escaping the room he had me locked away in and running towards the tree line.

My dad and Levi gave their statements and showed them where Tommy's guns were. They took pictures and bagged them as evidence. They needed my dad's gun and also Levi's, which was my dad's. They said they could have them back when the case closed. Officer John said he hoped I could find closure now. And that I felt safe. I told him I'd feel safe once I was out of here and was at home with everyone who loved me. We were there for about an hour, maybe a little more. I needed a shower and food.

Finally, they let us leave. I told Levi to please stop at that old lady's house. So, we did. I knocked on the door. Levi was with me, and my dad was in the car. "Hello, ma'am," I said. "Hello," she said back. "I don't know if you remember this guy, Levi." And Levi stepped up higher on the porch. "Oh, yes. Yes I do." She said, "Are you the girlfriend he was looking for?" "Yes, I am," I replied. "I wanted to thank you for talking to Levi and giving the description of the car and the backstory of who lives in that house down the way." I continued. "That's what made it possible for him to find me," I told her that I had been held captive for five or so days, but I escaped just as Levi was getting there.

She asked, "Is that what all the shooting was about, then the sirens." "Yes," I replied. The man who abducted me had two guns, and he was chasing me. Levi had a gun, and my dad who is currently in the car, had a rifle.

As I said that, my dad knocked on the door. "Who is that now?" she asked. "That's my dad," I said. "Come on in," she said. My dad walked in and thanked her for her help. He left his card with her and said if she ever needed help with anything, he would drop what he was doing and help her. "So basically, Levi told me how helpful you were, so I asked if I could stop and thank you myself before we head home." She said, "that was very sweet." "So, thank you again," I said.

I told her we needed to get going because my mom was at home probably going crazy. She said she could understand that. She said she was so happy that I was rescued. "What happened to the boy who lives there." she asked. "He is dead," I answered. "What a shame, she said. He doesn't sound at all like the boy I knew, but that was a long time ago," she said.

We said our goodbyes, and we all got in Levi's Jeep and headed to my house. I told my dad and Levi that they were my heroes! I couldn't believe they found Tommy's house! My dad called my mom when we were on the highway and had service. He tried calling her after he called the ambulance, but the service went out completely. He could barely hear her. He said we found Mac, but he had no idea if she heard. He was trying to call her in the Jeep before he came into the old lady's house but there was no service. "I can't believe I'm going home" I said loudly!

My dad tried calling my mom again once we had service. My mom answered and my dad said, "We have Mac. She's safe, and we are headed home." I could hear my mom squeal with excitement. I yelled, "I love you mom, see you soon!" She yelled back, I Love you, Mac!" Then I heard her tell whoever was at the house that I'd been rescued, and I was safe and on the way home!

We pulled up to the house, and before we even got out of the Jeep, everyone was on the front lawn. I hugged my mom first. Then, my sister, Michelle. I saw Mandi and Steve, and I gave them both a giant hug. I couldn't believe it. I saw Misty and Kaye, and I hugged them both. "We are on break, so we wanted to come here and wait on the news," they said. I collapsed to the ground, grabbed the grass, and laid down in the front yard.

"IT'S OVER!" I screamed as loud as I could.

Everyone was teary eyed and wanted all the details from the last five days, but Levi suggested, "Let's let Mac rest. She just had to kill a man and was held captive for five days trying to stay strong to get back to us. She needs to decompress. "You are absolutely right, Levi. Mac needs rest, we can talk whenever she is ready." My mom chimed in.

Hello, I'm sitting right here, I thought, laughing.

But I did need to decompress some. I'd been through hell, but I survived it. After nearly two years, it was finally over. I'm not sure I'll ever feel that way, but I'll keep telling myself it's over as many times as it takes.

We all went inside, and my dad turned on the news. And there it was, the desolate area and Tommy's house. Tommy was in a black bag and on a stretcher, being put in the back of the ambulance. Officer John was sharing some of what happened with the news. I was shocked. But I guess eventually my story is going to get out. And I didn't care anymore. I was safe and I was free!

It's really over this time! It's over.

About Stalking

Stalking is a serious issue that can turn lives upside down. This behavior, where someone persistently follows or harasses another person, must be addressed with urgency and understanding. Recognizing the impact of stalking on victims is essential for creating safer communities and supporting those in need.

Stalking can have devastating effects on the mental health of victims. Many people experience anxiety, depression, and fear as a result of being stalked. For example, consider the case of a young woman who received constant messages and unwanted visits from an ex-partner. Her daily life was filled with worry, making going to work or meeting friends difficult. This situation illustrates how stalking can take away a person's sense of safety and control, leading to long-lasting emotional scars.

Moreover, stalking can disrupt the victim's professional and personal life. When someone feels threatened, they often change their routines and avoid places they once enjoyed. This change can lead to isolation and difficulties in maintaining relationships. For instance, a man who was stalked by a coworker found it hard to concentrate at work. He avoided the office and missed important meetings, which affected his career. This example shows how stalking can not only harm individuals but also impact workplaces and communities.

In addition, raising awareness about stalking can help prevent it from happening. Many people do not understand what stalking is and may not recognize the signs. By educating communities about the dangers and warning signs of stalking, it becomes easier to take action. Schools, workplaces, and local organizations can play a vital role in spreading information and creating safe environments. When people know what to look for, they can support victims and report stalkers before the situation escalates.

In conclusion, stalking is a serious issue that can cause significant harm to victims. The emotional toll, disruption to everyday life, and the need for awareness highlight the importance of addressing this problem. Supporting victims and educating communities about stalking can lead to safer spaces for everyone. It is crucial to take action against stalking, ensuring that no one has to live in fear.

SPARC (Stalking Prevention, Awareness, & Resource Center) stalkingawareness.org,

Victim Connect: 1-855-484-2846 (1-855-4VICTIM)

National Domestic Violence Hotline: 1-800-799-7233

The National Sexual Assault Hotline: 1-800-656-4673 (1-800-656-HOPE)

According to Jessica Hanly on the Department of the Army Criminal Investigations Division (cide.army.mil} website, her article talks about Stalking Awareness. From her article, "Stalking

Awareness: Know the Signs and How to Respond," she talks about some examples of stalking.

- Unwanted following and watching of the victim.

- Unwanted approaching or showing up in places.

- Unwanted use of Global Positioning Systems 'GPS" Technology to monitor or track the victim's location.

- Leaving strange or potentially threatening items for the victim to find.

- Sneaking into the victim's home or car and doing things to scare the victim or let the victim know the perpetrator had been there.

- Use of Technology for example hidden camera, recorder, computer software, to spy on the victim from a distance.

- Unwanted phone calls, including hang-ups and voice messages

- Unwanted texts, emails, social media, or photo messages

- Unwanted cards, letters, flowers, or presents.

According to Jessica's article, anyone can become a stalking victim. Typically, victims are stalked by someone they know, such as an acquaintance, a former partner, or even a family member. The National Partner and Sexual Violence Survey (NISVS) reports that about one in three women and one in six men have been stocked at some point in their lives CDC website.

On "FighterLaw.com," they list the 10 signs that you are being stalked. I really liked these examples.

1. **Repetitive phone calls**– if you've noticed repeated requests from the same number or blocked number, it could be someone with damaging intentions. These types of people will try to "hear your voice" or call you repeatedly to act on the fantasies of speaking to you

2. **Constantly lurking around your home or workplace**– if you notice someone is showing up around your workplace, when you know they don't work there, as well as in your neighborhood, you're likely dealing with a deranged individual.

3. **Inappropriate gifts**– repeatedly receiving gifts from someone you don't know well is an uncomfortable experience, you know when it's inappropriate to get a gift, so this should put you on alert

4. **"Rescuing" You**–If you're on the road and your tire blew out, be wary of anyone that immediately pops up to help you fix it. That person may be neurotically finding ways to be in your presence, including sabotaging your well-being.

5. **Manipulating you into interacting**—We have a tendency toward politeness and Society, and sometimes those with delusional disorders use that to force you to talk to them. for example, cornering you at a party despite you making several hints

that you'd like to get away from them. They'll try to approach you somewhere where you can't say no or can't make a scene.

6. **Weird messages online**–With the internet, stalking is easier than ever. Pay close attention to your friends and followers on social media. Too many blank accounts following you could be a stalker. If you block them, they'll likely make several accounts to try speak to you again.

7. **Unwanted contact**–They might rub up on you in the street, consistently touch your arm or shoulders during conversations, or make themselves comfortable with you despite your objections.

8. **Trying to find out your plans**– A more obvious sign of stalking is to pay attention to who is asking too many questions about your whereabouts. Sometimes tailing you will try to sound natural by asking you what your plans are for the evening, or where you are going with your friend this weekend. A perfectly polite inquiry can have a hidden purpose.

9. **Alienation** –Another common behavior for those with stalkers, they will try to alienate you from your friends and family by telling lies or spreading rumors about you.

10. **Showing up unannounced**–If a person repeatedly comes to your home or work without you asking them to, they're likely there to check up on you.

About the Author

Hello! I'm Jenn, and I wear many hats. I'm a complex person with my share of flaws, but I've also lived through some incredible—and sometimes terrifying—experiences. Isn't that part of being human? I'm a Christian, a wife, and a mother of two, always striving to grow in my faith.

My hobbies have evolved over the years, though a few have stayed constant. I've always loved collecting coins, currency, rocks, and crystals. Horseback riding and volunteering are close to my heart, and I also enjoy knife-throwing, darts, and target practice. Art is a passion—I paint and create alcohol ink art, make jewelry, and refinish furniture. I also take on home projects and renovations whenever I can.

I run my own organizing business, and there's nothing I enjoy more than helping clients transform their spaces. Family time is precious to me; we love movie nights, bike rides, shopping trips, and getting ice cream together. Writing has also become a newfound love, along with heights—I've always felt a thrill from being up high. Maybe it's the view, maybe it's the adrenaline; whatever it is, I miss the rooftops I used to climb as a kid. Now, I find my peace relaxing on our trampoline, soaking in the sun.

Journaling eventually led me to write books, using my own experiences as inspiration. Writing has become my voice, a way to process, share, and maybe help others—or at least provide a bit of entertainment.

Made in the USA
Las Vegas, NV
07 November 2024